GOIN' FOR IRON

Sam Chapman stood by the saloon's batwings, taking in the two men confronting one another at a back card table and then glanced at the stranger standing near the front end of the long bar. The man had unleathered his Smith & Wesson and was holding it low by his side. Sam swung toward the bar and muttered quietly, "Two against one don't seem fair."

The man blinked in surprise.

"I'm not wearing this badge to ward off evil spirits," Sam went on. "Just ease that Smith & Wesson you're holding up on the bar or suffer the consequences."

"And if I don't?"

Sam jerked his thumb toward Joe McVay who was taking in what was happening at the bar and by the poker table. "His name's McVay. One of my deputies. All he knows is killing. Meaning that while you're thinking about where to shoot me or if the light is about right in here or anything else . . . all he has on his mind is blowing your lights out. Any other questions?"

GUNS ALONG THE YELLOWSTONE
ROBERT KAMMEN

ZEBRA BOOKS
KENSINGTON PUBLISHING CORP.

ZEBRA BOOKS

are published by

Kensington Publishing Corp.
475 Park Avenue South
New York, NY 10016

First printing: December, 1989

Printed in the United States of America

For Carol and Walt, and
for Auld Lang Syne . . .

Chapter One

Sam Chapman was on the long side of forty before he figured out that manual labor wasn't the president of Mexico. This revelation came after years of drifting and three broken marriages, two common law, but his first to an unsoiled dove over at Ekalaka. Often when in his cups Samuel Tyler Chapman would narrate in sonorous tones just how the belle of Ekalaka had trapped him into marriage. But in his drunken tellings Sam left out such vital parts as he hadn't been the first to bed Charlotte Pennymaker, that upon finding herself in a family way, she'd pointed the finger of blame at Sam Chapman instead of a Lazy T cowpoke. Whereupon frontier justice, Charlotte's rightful pa, the town marshal, had at gunpoint brought them before a Baptist preacher.

"Sam, about time you quit flimflamming us about all them doves you soiled."

"Well, Sam can sure as hell soil me," yelled a dusky-skinned whore named Lolita.

"That happens," retorted Mag Burns, "and you'll find yourself looking down the barrel of my Greener."

It was no secret around town that Mag Burns had gone soft on Sam Chapman. Mag ran one of the more fashionable parlor houses in Miles City. The *Yellowstone Journal* described Mag Burns as a handsome woman in her early thirties, with coiffured black hair, and easy smile, and that she generally wore long gowns that revealed her ample bosom. The same article went on to tell of how Mag had distributed engraved invitations at the formal opening of her hook shop. Her place became known as the 44, the figures being painted on the glass above the front door. And all because a bunch got down there buying drinks, and with Mag Burns saying she would name the place for the one buying the most rounds.

"Simmer down, Mag," said Sam Chapman as he smiled into her eyes still throwing out sparks.

"I'll try."

"I see you've got yourself some spanking new velvet curtains; red as hell though."

"Enough about my curtains, Sam. Just want to say I'm proud of you."

"Yup," shouted a leather-lunged cowpuncher, "U.S. Marshal Sam Chapman has a nice ring to it. That right, boys!"

A big, longlimbed man, Sam Chapman was all too conscious of the badge pinned to his leather vest. Months ago, or when campaigning really took a serious turn up here in Custer County, Sam had thrown in his lot with Judge Harlan A. Garth and other Republicans running for office. In his role as ward heeler, Sam Chapman went about canvassing votes along with soliciting small contributions. A lot of folks remarked that Sam could talk the husk off an ear of corn, that he was chiefly responsible for Judge Garth being reelected and Toby Pindale taking over as county sheriff. At the very most Sam had expected to get some mundane job up at the courthouse — either as county clerk or tax collector. So he hadn't been overly excited when Judge Garth had summoned him to his office at the courthouse. This all changed when he arrived there and the judge said boldly,

"Chapman, I've just been elevated to the federal bench. Meaning that I'm now the new federal judge for this part of territorial Montana. With a mandate to clean up this rustling."

"I reckon congrat . . ."

The next thing Sam Chapman knew the judge had tossed a marshal's badge across his spacious oaken desk to bark out, "You've earned that, Chapman."

"Me? I ain't no lawman."

"You are now."

A few hours and several drinks later, Sam Chapman was still somewhat shocked over Judge Garth's decision to make him a starpacker. Not one to harbor afterthoughts, or regrets over what a lot of folks had gotten to calling a wasted life, Sam couldn't help going back a lot of years to his yonker time. And to his pa, Shadrock Chapman, always harking that his only son was just too mouthy for his own good. There'd always, it seemed, been in Sam Chapman this passion for oratory. Many a time he'd talked himself out of trouble. Or out of one tight spot and into another. But when he needed words most they'd stayed lodged in his throat, and as a result he was being lauded by chance acquaintances and friends because he was now gainfully employed.

"What do you have planned for later, Sam?"

As another glass of cold beer was shoved into his hand, Sam Chapman said, "Just you and me in that big fourposter?"

"You asking or telling?"

"Mag, you know me. I've always been a gentleman."

"Right about now a very drunken one."

"Let's"—he slid an arm around Mag's shoulders—

"divest ourselves of these folks for a minute." He brought her through the press and beyond a beaded curtain into an anteroom. Stepping away from Mag Burns, he went to a window and gazed through elm trees at the darkening sky. Into Sam's light blue eyes came this reflective glimmer. "That election was too close for comfort."

"Garth's being elected judge left a bitter taste in a lot of mouths. So, Mr. Chapman, what's that got to do with you?"

"Hell, Mag, it was Garth's money that got him and Toby Pindale elected. Me—maybe I just wanted to be on the winning side for a change. But why this?"

She smiled at him, swinging to face her, and Mag said, "That badge becomes you."

"I lost a lot of friends when I supported the Republicans. This badge ain't gonna help my popularity any. What do I know about issuing warrants and such. The only time I've seen a cell is from the inside. Pindale now—or ex-sheriff Lawton—by rights Judge Garth should have given one of them this badge. Garth, dammit, he's up to something."

"Come on," said Mag, "you're always trying to find a skeleton in someone's closet. Judge Garth's no angel, I'll grant you that. But . . ."

"Neither is that wastrel of a son of his."

For a long time Sam Chapman had drifted in and out of Miles City. Though he could have hired on at any number of ranches, Sam kept avoiding that line of work, or anything that would tie him to taking orders from some bossman. Blackjack dealing was more in his line, poker, or presiding over a roulette wheel, and sometimes bardogging. The years hadn't been all that unkind to Sam Chapman, graying his hair along the temples, and giving him a tinge of gout; otherwise, for a man his age, the long face still retained a certain elegance and under the big Stetson lay a full head of dark brown hair.

In these wanderings he'd picked up assorted bits of information about then lawyer Harlan A. Garth, of how the man had left Chicago in search of adventure and a better life. It hadn't taken Garth long to line up a lot of clients or get himself appointed as state's attorney for Custer County. But it wasn't too long before folks began questioning the ethics of lawyer Garth. Nor wondering how a man coming here as he'd done without a whole lot of working capital could suddenly begin acquiring a lot of prime property, both in Miles City and some ranchland. Along with this, Harlan A. Garth had been active in the Republican Party. Out of this came Garth's winning in a close election the position of county judge.

Which brought Sam Chapman into pondering over how Judge Garth had somehow acquired ownership of the Clearwater Ranch. Its owner at that time, an old rancher named George Davine, had lost a lot of cattle to drought and the Indians. To keep his operations going Davine had borrowed heavily from the Citizens Bank of Miles City. One day the bank decided to foreclose, and in the ensuing legal battle the ranch was placed under receivership, this by Judge Harlan A. Garth. Then the sudden demise of rancher George Davine, some say under peculiar circumstances, saw the Clearwater Ranch being sold to Garth. Immediately he turned the ranch over to his son, Rydell Garth, but more commonly referred to as Rye. Only the judge pouring his money into the ranch kept it going, as Rye Garth seemed to spend most of his time at the gaming tables in Miles City or westward at Big Timber or Billings or Bozeman. To counteract this, Judge Garth had talked Phil Brady, a capable foreman over at the Slash L Ranch, into hiring on as manager

11

of the Clearwater. In less than six months the Clearwater had expanded its holdings considerably to become the largest spread between Miles City and the Judith Gap. Something that only caused more locals and ranchers to turn suspicious eyes upon their county judge.

In a way, Sam Chapman didn't expect Garth to win this recent election. But how badly, he was now realizing, had he underestimated what the man's political clout and money could do. With a wry grimace he brought the glass up and drank the rest of his beer.

"The judge said he was given a mandate to stop this rustling."

"Now, Sam," Mag Burns said around a teasing smile, "Any rustling you've ever done is for a drink, or to get the favors of a woman."

Despite his worried frame of mind, a grin inched up the corners of Sam's mouth. "This just means he was passing the buck. What in tarnation do I know about tracking down rustlers. Why, woman, even reading brands comes painful to me."

"I've seen men back down from you."

"Some drunks I caught cheating at cards is all, Mag. Wastrels who'd been so liquored up or afraid of losing at cards they couldn't tell their rear ends from the ace of spades. There's rustlers a-plenty out there; better men than me with a gun. And a lot of hostile Indians refusing to come in to the reservations. But red or white, all of them would like nothing better than to punch holes in this damned badge."

"Hell, Sam, give it back. I could always use another bouncer or bardog."

"You mean go ask Judge Garth for another job?"

"You don't have to wear that badge to prove you're a man."

"Guess I've proved that to you a heap of times, Mag Burns."

"Easy, Sam, you're too drunk for parlor games." She pushed his arm away. "Besides, we'd better get out there before they tear my place apart. Some friends you've got."

"Yup, better enjoy these free drinks whilst I still got some."

One of the barkeeps thrust his shoulders through the beaded curtain and said to Sam Chapman, "One of Garth's bailiffs is looking for you."

"First day on the job," groused Chapman, "and Garth pulls this on me." He handed the barkeep his empty glass and followed the man into the front living room where some of Mag's girls were entertaining the celebrants. Farther back was a barroom, and down a corridor a small gaming room, opposite that some rooms. And it was at the back end of the corridor that Sam Chapman found the bailiff, whose right hand still hovered near the door knob for fear one of the hookers would entice him upstairs. "Get to the shank of it, Jesson."

"The army's brought in some prisoners."

"Some more Injuns?"

"Them which killed those soldiers over by Mizpah Creek. Got 'em lodged in the county jail."

"So what's the problem then?"

"Judge Garth wants you pronto, Marshal Chapman."

"Well, dammit, Jesson, go tell the judge I'm too drunk to carry out any marshalling duties." He swung away.

"The judge'll be madder'n a bull moose about this."

"Tough," rasped Chapman. "Anyway, this just happens to be Sheriff Pindale's problem."

"Nope, Marshal Chapman. Ain't county business,

13

according to Judge Garth. It's federal — meaning you're to watch over them prisoners."

Sam Chapman stopped short and spun around. "Leave it to Garth to bury a man under legal jurisprudence. What about those soldier boys? They come under federal business."

"They left, once the prisoners were placed in cells."

"Still in chains I hope. Awright, tell the judge I'll wander over to the courthouse. After I've had another snifter of corn liquor."

"As you say, marshal."

"Whoa here now, Jesson. Ham Lauden's jailer — meaning Ham's supposed to watch over them Injuns."

"Only to see they're fed and make sure they don't despoil the cells."

"Sonofabitches can piss all over them cells for all I care."

"I hardly expect a U.S. Marshal to take that attitude."

"Bailiff, there's lawmakers and there's lawbreakers. Up to now this old hoss has been one of them lawbreakers, so to speak. Meaning this badge pinned to my chest is gettin' damned heavy. It just ain't my nature to wetnurse a bunch of Injuns. Why didn't them soldiers boys just up and hang them heathens."

"They must have a fair trial," the bailiff said curtly.

"Meaning more of Judge Garth's legal jurisprudence."

"I suggest you hire some deputy marshals."

"That's what the judge suggested I do. This morning after he stuck this badge into my chest. Be so kind as to tell Ham Lauden I'll be along shortly." He glared at the bailiff slipping out the door. The temptation was strong to head back to the drinking crowd, just forget going over to the courthouse. Sam reached up and thumbed his hat back as his eyes narrowed

14

thoughtfully. So far, son, you've been playing the fool. Nobody cares about a drifter, much less one edging onto his fifties. Give this marshal's job a fair shake, or at least until you find out why Judge Garth handed you this badge.

"Darnation," Sam Chapman groused as he swung open the back door and found the dark alleyway, "ever since I started thinking I was a Republican, life has sure got complicated. Just hope politics don't prove to be my undoing."

Chapter Two

Sam Chapman always seemed to get this itchy feeling whenever he chanced to pass a jail or any other law enforcement building. Over the passage of a few years he'd traced the source of this problem to the harsh treatment laid upon him by badgepackers. Sam's malady was twofold. As a sometime gambler, this in localities he entered as a stranger, more often than not Sam would cash in a lot of chips. Being larger than most and packing at his right hip that .45 Peacemaker, he could amble out peaceable. Only to be confronted by a local lawman wanting in on the gambling action. Sometimes it would mean incarceration. Most often he'd find himself riding out of town stone broke and shaking away an itch or two.

Now Sam could feel a slight twinge when he turned the corner and stared at the three story brick courthouse dominating a city block. Light splashing out of a second story window told him Judge Garth was still in his office. Garth had a reputation for putting in long hours, even coming in on Sundays when he had a full docket. But let the judge wait, mused Sam, as he went in the front door and found a stairway running down to the cell block. There were five cells on either side of a narrow corridor, but before that

17

was a small room occupied by jailer Ham Lauden.

"That coffee stale?"

"Oh, Chapman. About time you showed up."

"I don't know why," Sam muttered. "What's the rundown on your prisoners?"

"The army brought in five of them, Northern Cheyenne. A waste of time since they'll be hung anyway." Ham Lauden had wide sloping shoulders and faded bib overalls covered his stout frame. Though possessed of a taciturn manner, Lauden had a sly sense of humor. Some folks got nettled at Ham Lauden because at times they couldn't decide if he'd just cracked a joke or was dead serious. "You ought to have seen the look on Kiley Glover's face when them Cheyenne came trooping in."

"He in jail again?"

"Uh-huh, Glover and his bunch. Got them lodged in the last cell on the right; that way Kiley'll get a better view of the gallows."

"The charge breaking and entering again?"

"This time Glover is suspected of going bigtime — charged with stealing horses."

"What the hell does suspected mean?"

"He was seen in the vicinity."

A disdainful snort came from Sam Chapman. "Just like when I'm playing five card stud. I always suspect the other players are holding a whole passel of aces. Been proved right most of the time. Getting back to them Cheyenne, they secured properly?"

Now it was Ham Lauden's turn to register a little disdain. "They're still decorated with handcuffs asides having their ankles chained to a bull-ring lodged in the floor. Even if this place catches fire, Sam, I ain't gonna take them irons off."

"You always did have a Christian attitude regarding Injuns and half-bloods."

"Reason I've still got some hair. Wanna hear what them Cheyenne done?"

Sam Chapman said that he did.

The sad tale of how these Northern Cheyenne came to be here began when Black Coyote, an unruly warrior in his band, killed two men in a camp quarrel and was banished. His wife, the famous Buffalo Calf Woman who had rescued her brother, Comes-in-sight, in the battle of the Rosebud, and a few relatives elected to follow the outcast into exile. When in the vicinity of Mizpah Creek, this band of renegades came upon two soldiers working on the Fort Keogh-Deadwood telegraph line. They severely wounded one of the soldiers, killed the other, and stole their horses. A few days later they were captured by a small detail of the 2nd Cavalry. As the case was adjudged to be of a civil nature, Black Coyote and the other warriors were brought here so that their case could be handled by the new territorial court.

"An interesting story, don't you think, Chapman?"

Marshal Sam Chapman lowered the tin cup to the cluttered table and turned to grimace at the man who'd given him this new job. In doing so Sam had to lower his gaze some, for Harlan A. Garth was a short and lean man garbed in an eastern suit, charcoal in color. The eyes told Sam all he had to know about Judge Garth. They were black unsmiling orbs in a thin horsey face. Unlike jailer Lauden, the new territorial judge didn't have a sense of humor, and it was Sam's opinion that Garth took life far too seriously. You never saw the man in the bars, or for that matter, out enjoying Miles City's rather boisterous nightlife. Another thing that Sam didn't particularly like about the judge was how the black hair was parted in the middle and folded to either side, neatly so that each strand lay just right. Fastidious, that was the word. And he'd even lay odds the man had his underwear starched and ironed. Just maybe, Sam pondered, he'd take a stroll over to Li Chan's Laundry and check this out.

"It all depends if you're red or white skinned. What about the squaws and kids?"

"They were sent down to the reservation of the Southern Cheyenne. And good riddance to them. Come, Chapman, I'll show you to your office."

"Obliged for the chitchat, Ham."

With some reluctance Sam Chapman trudged behind the judge up the narrow staircase. Then down a first floor corridor to be conducted into a small room. Sitting behind the only desk was, Sam recalled, one of Judge Garth's clerks, a seedy individual named Otis Plumb. Plumb surveyed the world and the new marshal through lens so thick they made his eyes look big as turkey eggs. Around a curt nod he kept on shuffling papers. There was barely room for the oak filing cabinets and a couple of chairs and a brass cuspidor.

"Since you'll be spending most of your time out hunting down criminals, Chapman, any paperwork will be handled by Otis."

Which was a plain way of saying Otis Plumb was here to keep tabs on the new marshal, and in Sam came this stirring of resentment. Already the room was giving him this closed in feeling, that, and an itch along his jawline. The positive side of this arrangement was that he could learn something about the law from Plumb. But Plumb didn't have to tell him a darn thing about being arrested. That was a procedure he had down cold. Arresting someone for a change instead of being the arrestee might be a whole new cup of tea.

"So I've got myself a paper shuffler, Judge Garth. What about deputy marshals?"

"Your responsibility. Put an ad in the *Yellowstone Journal*. But you'll need some in the next couple of days, Chapman. To watch over those Cheyenne when I haul them into my courtroom. Any questions?"

"Where do you take a leak around this brick monstrosity?"

Judge Harlan A. Garth shoved past his new marshal and found the door.

It didn't take Marshal Chapman more than a day to place that ad in the *Yellowstone Journal*. Afterward he went around town looking up men who might be interested in getting into the law business. He even had time to visit the 44. And it was here while sipping a cold beer with Mag Burns that someone came in to tell them another murder had been committed.

"One of Annie Turner's girls?"

"They found her down by the river. All cut up like that."

The madam in question had a house over in Coon Row, behind which were a string of shacks frequented by her whores. About every night there was a fight or someone got knifed. This was a place that Sam Chapman shied away from, and he knew the killing would be forgotten within the week had it not been for other girls getting murdered.

21

"Obviously someone doesn't like women," commented Mag Burns.

"Shouldn't you be doing something about this, marshal?"

"I was told flat out that Sheriff Toby Pindale is the law here in Miles City."

"Maybe it's just as well, Sam, since you don't know a damn thing about marshaling." The man who'd said that allowed a snicker to widen his bewhiskered mouth.

"I'm looking for deputies, Claybourne."

"What you need backing you is the 2nd Cavalry; every man jack of them."

Despite the fact Sam was getting a little nettled, he managed to say pleasantly, "I sure wouldn't turn them down."

"Sam, we need to talk."

"I hear you." Pushing up from his chair, Sam followed Mag Burns over to a back table. But she went past the table to a window and stared out at the late afternoon sun.

"What do you make of it?"

"Of that girl getting killed," responded Sam. "It happens."

"One at Big Timber, before that at Bozeman, and now here."

"Seems to me, Mag, you're trying to tie these killings into a neat bundle."

"One of them worked for me, Bess Rydel. You know how it is, my girls get the urge to travel, they hit the circuit."

Sam knew that girls of the demimonde, a word he'd picked up from the *Yellowstone Journal*, floated from one town to another—Cheyenne, Deadwood, Miles

City, Billings, and Helena. Others became residents of a sort but with some of the characteristics of migrant workers. These women gave a wide berth to the Seventh Commandment, but even so a number of them had admirable qualities. This was a woman-poor society and many men, because of their boozing and reckless habits, were shunned by the few "respectable" women. And so, like Sam Chapman, they sought female companionship at the dance halls and parlor houses. Those who married acquired respectability for, according to the code out here, no one dared speak ill of them after they broke with the profession. There were some women of the profession, such as Mag Burns, who often loaned hard cash to men down on their luck.

"Sam, it could have been one of my customers."

"Could have been, Mag. I'll have a talk with Sheriff Pindale."

"Pindale's not concerned with those other murders. But I checked them out. Both of those girls were mutilated . . . whoever did it used a knife to carve up their faces, cut them almost to the belly. Sam, the same thing could happen to one of my girls. To tell you the truth, I'm scared."

"Just to play it safe, Mag, you'd better tell your girls to start packing guns."

Mag Burns's smile cleared the worry from her eyes. "That could be awful hard at certain times."

"Maybe we're coming onto hard times now that Garth got himself reelected."

"What do you mean by that?"

"Don't know, Mag, just don't know. For starters he gave me this badge. With him knowing all about the workings of the law, reckon I just won't know when

Garth is flimflamming me. But it's a job . . . of sorts."

"Sam, you will talk to the sheriff." She reached out and brushed her hand along his cheek.

"Generally I get a kiss."

"That'll happen after you talk to the sheriff."

"Sooner than you think, Mag."

Chapter Three

"Come on, Chapman, there's no connection between those other murders. Besides . . ."

"Yup, Sheriff Pindale, she was one of the demimonde," he said scornfully. "Just another whore."

"These harlots live hard and die harder. You know that, Sam. Despite what you think," said Toby Pindale, "I went over to Annie Turner's place and questioned her girls. But when it comes to lawmen, they're awful short on answers. Sam, you can tell Mag Burns I'll keep checking into it." They were standing on a shady corner of the Cosmopolitan Theatre, a variety house on the south side of Main Street at 6th Street. Pindale started to turn away.

"There's something else, Toby."

Stopping short, the sheriff of Custer County cast a questioning glance over his shoulder.

"Maybe you could tell me why Judge Garth left town so suddenly—"

"Figure he went out to the Clearwater spread."

"Meaning his wastrel of a son got himself in trouble again."

"That's a touchy subject with the judge, Sam. Keep harping on it and Judge Garth might be looking for another marshal." This time Toby Pindale kept on going.

He could have expected as much from Pindale, a man Judge Garth had handpicked to be the next sheriff of Custer County. Before this Toby Pindale rode shotgun on the Bismark to Miles City stagecoach, and there was a brief stint as a deputy sheriff. In that capacity Pindale had enforced writs and foreclosures signed by Judge Harlan A. Garth. But judging Pindale's character, Sam had Toby pinned as being somewhat dull-witted but honest.

Just up the street Sam found Charlie Brown's saloon. At the crowded bar he took the cold stein of beer he'd paid for and a plateful of free lunch, bologna, cheese and beans, to an out-of-the-way table. He was in no mood for socializing or turning aside snide remarks. So far there'd only been one lonely response to his ad in the *Yellowstone Journal*. None as far as Sam Chapman was concerned, for he'd discounted an old sot of a buffalo hunter named Fargo Brisbie as a candidate for deputy marshal.

"Supporting the Republicans," muttered Sam, "wasn't the smartest thing I've ever done." He forked into the beans and began eating.

"May I join you?"

Sam turned sour eyes up at Otis Plumb hovering over his table, and grudgingly he said, "Why not — nothing else has gone right."

After Otis heaved the chair closer to the table and propped his elbows on it, he said, "I've heard that you haven't been too successful in your hunt for deputies."

"You come to gloat or what?"

26

—"Legally, Marshal Chapman, you have the right to hire about anybody in an emergency as your deputy, or deputies."

"Meaning I should trot out to boot hill and dig up some remains . . ."

"There are four outlaws taking their ease in your jail right now."

"First of all, Otis Plumb, that jail belongs to Custer County. And . . . and making deputy marshals out of them could see me stretched out in a pine box. Unless . . ." Sam's narrowed eyes peered back at Otis Plumb over the rim of his glass.

"Readers can be printed up on them."

"Yeah, and sent to places they might go and have been. Make them charges strong enough, Otis."

"I expect rustling and murder will do."

"Just to make them stronger, throw in wife beating. By the by, Mr. Plumb. why all this sudden concern for old Sam Chapman?"

"Let's just say that the presence of those Northern Cheyenne tends to unsettle my nerves."

"Reckon that'll do for starters, Otis."

To clear the stuffiness out of his new office, Sam Chapman had ordered Otis Plumb to leave the windows open, and through them now swept a summery breeze and dying sunlight. Otis had since departed for home.

Sam found that the padded chair behind his desk fitted his large frame. His spurred boots were propped on it as was a bottle of Carstair's Best and a tray holding some shot glasses, while he'd been sipping from one. Flavoring the air was smoke from

Sam's cigarette, the filling in it a special blend of Mex tobacco he'd gotten into the habit of buying over at Raskin's Smoke Shop & Billiard Emporium. During his idling days, less than a week ago as a matter of public record, daytimes would find him there either besting others at call shot or nine ball or hunkered at a poker table. That was a life he'd savored to the fullest.

"Wonder if being gainfully employed will be all that fun," Sam questioned as he reached over to the gunrack and lifted out a Greener, for he'd just picked up the sound of rattling chains and heavy steps on the stairway running up from the Basement Felony. As he waited, Sam made no attempt to load the heavy weapon, but he did refill his empty glass.

"Marshal Chapman!" boomed out jailer Ham Lauden.

"Bring the prisoner in!"

A boot in Kiley Glover's back sent the outlaw tumbling into the room. He slammed into a wooden cabinet and grunted in pain. Then Ham Lauden was there to lift the manacled prisoner to his feet and onto a chair resting before the marshal's desk. Stepping away, Lauden stationed himself near the open door.

Both Kiley Glover's wrists and ankles were bound by irons. And he'd brought a pungent body odor into the room. Glover's shaggy light brown hair tufted away from his skull. He was lean to the point of being skinny, not as tall as Sam, but possessed of lean arms and legs. Stubble lay thick on his angular jawline and his upper lip mustache needed trimming. The long nose of Kiley Glover rode slightly

28

to his left, the eyes of a dull gray and filled with a need to know what in tarnation was going on.

"I expect by now, Kiley, you're getting tired of looking at them gallows."

"Tired of being jailed for something I didn't do."

Below skeptical brows Sam reached over for a clipboard and began sheafing through the papers attached to it. "According to your arrest record, Kiley, that's what you claim everytime they find you. Let's see, breaking and entering, robbing a drunken buffer hunter, petty thievery, now rustling horses. Son, I can go on and on."

"I ain't your son."

"That's one thing I've got to be thankful for," snapped Sam, picking up his shot glass.

Sneered Kiley Glover, "Before you got to wearing that badge, Chapman, you was nothin' but a drunk and idler."

"True," grinned Sam Chapman. "Never will deny that."

"Marshal, you want me to scuff Glover up for being sarcastic?"

"Won't be necessary, Ham, from the looks of that shiner he's getting."

Kiley Glover rattled his wrist chains. "Get to it, Chapman, just why in tarnation did you fetch me here?"

"Because of my concern for your health."

"That'll be a sorry day," jeered the outlaw.

"Son, you might as well know," Sam said grimly. "Judge Garth wants you hung . . . and soon. Maybe within the week."

"But they didn't find us with them horses!" protested Kiley Glover, and this time fear shone brightly in his eyes to drive away some of the dullness.

"Don't make no difference." Sam shuffled the papers. "The rancher signed these charges. Judge Harlan A. Garth just told me, son, a long trial won't be necessary. It only takes less'n a minute to say 'Guilty As Charged!' Hangman's due here tomorrow, Kiley. But remember, you won't die alone. Guess you'll enjoy hanging alongside your friends."

Kiley Glover's mouth twisted up and his eyes dropped to show more white, which was about the color of his taut face, and then he began sobbing and sort of whimpering, to which Sam Chapman drained his glass again.

Winking at Ham Lauden, Marshall Chapman dropped this saving morsel, "But there is a way to save your mangy hide, Kiley."

It took a moment for what Sam had just uttered to get through to the outlaw, and then Glover mumbled, "There is? You know, Marshal Chapman, I don't wanna get hung."

"Nobody does, son." Sam filled his glass again and another one for Kiley Glover. "Here, Kiley, this might brace up your backbone. Ham?"

"Could use a drink." Ham Lauden shuffled forward.

"Here's my proposition, Kiley Glover. What it boils down to is that you'll be doing honest work for a change . . . lawmen's work."

"Don't follow you none?"

Dropping his legs to the floor, Sam opened a drawer and pulled out a badge which he dropped onto his desk. "I'm needing some deputy marshals."

"You . . . you mean . . . me pin on that thing?"

30

"It won't bite you none, Kiley."

"Me, a lawman?"

"You and Mort Reiser and Chili Tugwell and Joe McVay."

"Us . . . enforcing the law? Is this some kind of joke?"

"Ask Ham Lauden."

"I was you, Glover, I'd listen right smart to the marshal. For it don't matter none to me if you get strung up alongside the others or them mangy Injuns."

"Come on, Chapman, what's the catch?"

"You'll be sworn in as U.S. deputy marshals. Reporting only to me. You'll receive a dueful wage . . . your weaponry will be paid for . . . as will your horses. I've been given a mandate to go after rustlers, Kiley. Perhaps some old acquaintances of yours. That being the case, I expect you to do your duty as a deputy marshal. Either that or you'll be hung by your mangy neck until you're dead."

"You sure do paint a rosy picture. But what choice do I have?"

"None."

"But just pondering, Chapman, me and my gang being out there with just you. What's to stop us from just up and blowing your lights out and cutting out someplace?"

Dropping the remains of his cigarette and putting the flame out with the heel of his boot, Sam removed from the clipboard a sheet of paper and turned it so Kiley Glover could see that it was a newly printed reader.

"That's me . . . and Joe . . . and the others? Wanted for rustling and murder? Dammit, Chapman, that's a bold-faced lie! I might have wounded some, but never killed nobody . . . at least not up to now. And . . . and wife beating? None of us have ever got close to being hitched. These are bold-faced lies!"

"Son," Chapman said flatly, "these readers have been sent to all law enforcement agencies within a thousand miles, and maybe beyond that. You and Joe and Mort'll be safe long's you don't drift out of territorial Montana . . . which in my estimation means Custer County. Westward, there's another U.S. marshal at Bozeman, and he just might take unkindly to your presence just in case you ever drifted that far."

Kiley Glover's chains rattled as he lurched to his feet. "I knew there was a catch to all your sweet-talk, Chapman. And that picture of us on that reader . . . yeah, it was taken day before yesterday when that photographer from the *Yellowstone Journal* just chanced to drop by. Just a-setting us up, Chapman, was all you was doing!"

"Want me to rattle his chains some more?"

"Nope, Ham, won't be necessary. Take Mr. Glover back to his cell so's he can keep an eye out case someone steals our gallows. Here, son, might as well have this whiskey."

"Obliged for nothing."

"I'll be wanting an answer come sunup, Kiley."

"Expect you do," the outlaw said sarcastically.

"Oh, another thing. Ham, the hangman checked into the Calumet Hotel this afternoon. He'll be dropping by wanting to get a look at these rustlers."

"You mean to get an idea of their body weight to gauge what kind of knots to make on his hanging ropes."

"Sure wouldn't want these boys to suffer unjustly once they began that sudden drop."

Chapter Four

The Clearwater Ranch took up a sizable hunk of land along the Tongue River. It ran south to the Northern Cheyenne Agency and west of the river as far as Rosebud Creek. Once in a while a few renegade Cheyenne would steal some cattle, but mainly to slaughter and eat. More than once Judge Harlan Garth had sent his son, Rye, down to the agent at Lame Deer in an attempt to end this rustling. Then for a while, a couple of weeks or a month at the most, things would calm down.

This was a situation that Judge Garth felt he could handle. But of greater concern were the reports coming in to his courthouse at Miles City. This time the rustlers were gangs of white men. They operated out of any number of mountain ranges, the Pryor, Big Belts, Judith. Other hideouts infested by these rustlers lay among the flood plains of the main rivers. Oftentime they operated with impunity, simply because lawmen were still a scarce commodity in a place just wrested from the grasp of the Plains Indian.

This was not, however, why Harlan Garth had left Miles City so abruptly. The death of that harlot had caused him to saddle up his gelding and head out for the Clearwater. That had been three days ago. But upon reaching the main buildings, he'd been told by segundo Phil Brady that his son was off someplace. The only thing he could do now had been to wait for Rye Garth to show up. Then, earlier this morning, one of those who'd been hired more for his gunhandling abilities than ranch work had returned to find the owner of the Clearwater waiting for him.

"Aren't you Waddell?"

"Yessir, Judge Garth," the gunhand said through tight lips. He swung down.

"Tend to his horse," the judge told Phil Brady. "You, Waddell, come with me." He brought the gunhand into the main house and back to the office he shared with his son.

The gunhand had been hired on about a year after he'd acquired the Clearwater. The job of Waddell and two others of his breed was that of bodyguards for Rye Garth. This was the excuse Judge Garth used to keep these men on the payroll. But only Harlan Garth knew the true reason. For lodged in him was this strange feeling that someday he would be charged with the murder of George Davine, the man who'd started this ranch. That killing had been done by a hired gun out of Oklahoma. And if he was found out, Harlan Garth knew he would need men like Waddell again.

Of more pressing importance to Harlan Garth at the moment was a recurrence of what had happened, years ago it seemed, back in Chicago. Then the murderer had been his son, Rye. A couple of street walkers had been found, on different nights, with their faces slashed to ribbons. In a large place like the Windy City the death of a whore only took up a couple of lines on the back pages of its newspapers.

36

One day a homicide detective had shown up at his lake front office. Garth was told that his son had been arrested; the charge was first-degree murder.

"You've got a nice plush layout here, Mr. Garth," the detective went on. "Probably takes a lot of wealthy clients to keep an office like this up. And maybe you've got a lot of money stashed away in the banks. Too bad that it'll be over soon—for you and your son."

"What do you mean?"

"Your son didn't just kill those whores, Mr. Garth. They were cut up something awful. Only a man with a sick mind could do something like that, maybe someone with a grudge against women . . . and whores in particular. I promised those lousy reporters they'd get a story this afternoon."

"I can probably guess why you came here first."

"You're a lawyer, Mr. Garth. Means you know what the score is. Why, if the price was right I could find a way to clear your son's name."

When Harlan Garth left Chicago a few weeks later it was with less than three hundred dollars to his name. During this time his son had steadfastly denied killing those women, that he'd been framed. At the time Harlan Garth had tried to believe that Rye was no murderer. A widower, he only had his twenty-year-old son and now a lot of bitter memories. Though somewhat short of hard cash, Harlan Garth still had that lawyer's knowledge, along with a new coldhearted attitude when he arrived in Miles City and set out his shingle. He found the people out here were more open and trusting, and he took advantage of this with a vengeance. In the seven years he'd been here, Judge Harlan Garth had become moderately wealthy. As for the Clearwater

Ranch, he first set eyes upon it on a buggy ride down there with the president of the Peoples Bank of Miles City. Along the way the banker detailed to him the financial difficulties rancher Davine was having. But once he viewed those buildings strung along the Tongue River, Harlan Garth knew that somehow he must acquire the Clearwater at any cost. Thus it became, through the murder of George Davine, his coup de main, his showcase.

Judge Harlan A. Garth had bore no grudge against rancher Davine. In a way he'd considered this purely a business transaction, when the man had been killed, and afterward through the legal process of law that had seen him gain control of the Clearwater. Afterward he could attend church with a clear conscience.

Then these senseless killings began. Though he kept telling himself his son had unbloodied hands, Harlan Garth knew Rye was behind this. He'd gone over to the undertaker's shabby place of business in Miles City and viewed the body. Sheriff Toby Pindale had been there, and together they'd more or less agreed that a drifter had killed the woman. Shortly after that Harlan Garth was on his way to the Clearwater.

Now he said angrily, "Where's my son?"

The gunhand, Waddell, said evasively, "Over at Sonnette. He sent me back to get some more money."

"Gambling again, I suspect. I want the truth now, Waddell. Were you up at Miles City within the last week—more specifically, three days ago."

"We've been a lot of places in the last week."

"Dammit, was my son in Miles City?"

"All of us where there."

"That'll be all," he said abruptly, and the gunhand

stepped out of the room.

Slamming his clenched fist down on the desk, Judge Garth struggled to control his growing anger. How long would it be before someone connected his son with these killings? Rye was well known at Miles City and other towns strung along the Yellowstone River. This madness that had taken control of his son could see both of them either dead or in jail.

Sonnette, he would have to go there and confront his son.

They came upon Pumpkin Creek shortly after sundown and brought their horses along it and to the south. The pair of cowhands acting as escort hadn't exchanged a civil word with Judge Garth ever since crossing the Tongue River around midday. By reputation they knew the judge to be tightlipped and tightfisted. These two, and other Clearwater waddies, were always keeping an ear peeled to news that other ranchers were hiring. But these were tough times and any kind of ranching job was hard to come by.

For a couple of miles they'd been lagging a short distance behind the judge holding that brown gelding of his to a canter. There was still plenty of sunlight piercing down from a reddish sky. The wind was just strong enough to keep away mosquitos which came sweeping up from river-weeds and reeds growing in the brackish waters. Just ahead of them stood a big oak tree, and with one of the cowhands whispering to the other,

"Bet the judge would sure like to hang Rye to that tree."

"For certain he's a ne'er-do-well. But I wouldn't want to call Rye that to his face."

"Not with those gunslicks hanging around."

"Never seen the judge this angry before."

"Just so's he don't take it out on us."

They followed Judge Garth down a dusty lane trekking into the little cowtown of Sonnette. A couple taking their ease on the front porch of their clapboard house waved, but both the judge and cowhands passed by without a glance. Coming onto a narrow street that didn't have any boardwalks, they drew up behind Judge Garth as he twisted in the saddle to look back at them.

"There's just the two saloons," he said curtly. "Don't want to see you boys in either one of them. I see Sander's trading post is still throwing out light; I'll meet you there shortly."

Then Harlan Garth brought his horse angling downstreet. He bypassed the first saloon since none of the horses tethered to the hitching racks wore the Clearwater brand. A woman came around the corner of the only grocery store and looked up at the judge riding by. The look on Judge Garth's face caused her to hurry into the store. The other saloon was set back from the street, and the judge reined toward it, with his eyes narrowing angrily when he spotted, among other horses tied there, the bay his son favored. After tying up, he stepped back and lifted a quirt out of a saddlebag. Passing his hand through the wrist-loop, he headed for the open doorway.

The barkeep saw the newcomer first, but Harlan Garth only had eyes for one of the gunhands slouched in a chair, his hat shoved to the back of his head and grunting between snores. There was nobody else in the place, and Garth caught the barkeep's eye and said quietly, "I assume you know Rye Garth?"

"There's a poker game going on back there." He nodded at one of the doors.

"How long has it been going on?"

"On and off for a couple of days."

"The fool never learns," he said more to himself. As he slipped around a table and went along the bar, a back door creaked open and the other gunhand who rode with his son came into the barroom, only to pull up short when he realized Judge Harlan A. Garth was there. "Don't bother telling my son I'm here. Go wake up Sundby; all three of you are heading back to the ranch."

"Tonight?"

"The ride'll sober you up. Now stand aside." He brushed past the gunhand and stepped into the smoke-clogged room. Only four men were seated around the poker table, Rye Garth, another cow-puncher, and the other men wore suits. The one having on a muley smiled up at the judge.

"We could sure use another player."

"The game's over, gents!"

The instant Rye Garth recognized his father's voice he shifted his chair sideways and started to rise. Confusion played in his reddened eyes. The smile he started framing was swept away by Harlan Garth's quirt lashing out to scatter poker chips and cards.

"Pa, I . . ."

"You others, clear the hell out of here! Now, dammit!"

The cowpuncher shoved his chair back in rising. "No man can talk to me like that."

"I'm Judge Harlan Garth . . . federal judge for territorial Montana . . . and I've just closed this game. Gather your money, gents, and clear out. All except you!" He speared his son with a killing stare. Then, when the others had gone into the barroom, he reached over and slammed the door shut. Almost in the same motion he lashed out with the quirt to catch Rye Garth in the face.

"Why?" He kept lashing out with the quirt as his son threw up an arm to protect his face and shoulders. "Why? What the hell is wrong with you to go around killing again!"

Under ordinary circumstances Rye Garth would be considered a ruggedly handsome man. But boozing had flushed his face and given him a slight paunch. He had the dark features of his father, though he was a few inches taller. The Stetson and long-sleeved shirt were a dark brown, the tan vest hung open, the gun at his right hip was a Smith & Wesson.

"Pa . . . what's this all about? I haven't killed anybody."

"Three harlots were murdered . . . as if you didn't know."

"I swear, pa, this is the first I knew of this. Sure . . . back there . . . in Chicago, they accused me of the same thing. But I was framed." Somehow he managed to get the table between them. "Same's as I'm being framed now. I swear, pa, on my mother's grave that I'm not involved in this."

"As you say," he said flintily. "For the next month or two I want you to stay clear of Miles City, those other towns. You could ruin everything I've worked for . . . and can get now that I'm a federal judge. You savvy, Rye Garth?"

Harlan Garth let the bitter anger slowly drain out of his system. The only thing he could do was order Rye to stay out at the Clearwater. Then if these killings continued he would know for certain his son was no murderer. Now he said bluntly, "You and the others find your horses and head right back to the ranch. And you stay put until I say different. I talked to your foreman, and Brady said he could use some help running the place."

"Might as well get started," Rye Garth said bitterly. "But I'll tell you this, my pa or no, you come at me with that quirt again, it'll be curtains for one of us."

Rye Garth hurried through the barroom and found his horse. He yanked hard on the reins to swing it away from the hitch rail, with his jabbing spurs setting the bay into a startled gallop. At the edge of town he slowed down to let the others catch up with him. There was still some lingering pain from the lashing his father had given him, and his left cheek had suffered a small cut.

"Sundby, ride on ahead. I'll catch up with you." Rye waited until Sundby was hidden by a copse of elm trees before he turned sullen eyes upon the other gunhand, Bilo Mackley, a thin-lipped Oklahoman.

"The judge has a bigger temper than yours, Rye."

"Sometimes," he had to admit.

"Does he know?"

"You're the only one who knows I killed that whore over at Miles City. It just . . . happens."

"Get to the shank of it—"

"A thousand dollars if you do a certain job for me, Bilo."

"A lot of money."

"You've killed before, so one more shouldn't ruffle your feathers none."

"The judge?"

"Tempting." Rye Garth laughed bitterly. "Awful damned tempting. To do this job you'll have to go to

43

Miles City."

"And kill who?"

"One of Mag Burns's whores."

Chapter Five

Kiley Glover and his cronies could scarcely believe they'd been let out of jail, much less become the possessors of deputy marshal badges. Miles City heard about this through front page headlines in the *Yellowstone Journal*. A lot of folks started talk that Marshal Sam Chapman should be fired. It got so that Sam could count on the fingers of one hand those he considered friends.

"To hell with 'em," me muttered. "Kiley, you and Chili Tugwell stand the first watch."

"You can depend on us, marshal."

"Hope so. You'll be relieved at midnight."

"This is a right pretty badge," commented Chili Tugwell. "Just wearing it makes me feel kind of important."

"Just don't let that badge dazzle you into getting careless. Chained and cuffed as they are, those Cheyenne are still dangerous."

"Well, if they was gonna hang me," said Kiley Glover, "I'd sure as hell try something."

"You did, Kiley."

"No comprendo, Sam?"

"What kept the judge from carrying out your hanging sentence was you becoming a deputy. Just remember that. Anyway, my stomach's growling." Sam headed for the door. "Figure on me being back later."

Alone, the new deputy marshals settled down around the desk and began playing gin, along with ragging over just how long they'd have to endure being lawmen before cutting out someplace. Glover said, "Those readers Sam put out on us will sure cramp our style."

"What about when we take out after rustlers."

"Yup, we've got a lot of old friends out there. Somehow it just don't seem natural going after them."

"Out there covers a lot of territory."

Just this afternoon they'd been given a briefing by their new bossman, as to what was expected of them as deputy marshals. Along with being shown a map of the territory under Marshal Chapman's jurisdiction. Firstly, Miles City was the county seat of Custer County, but which had originally been called Big Horn County. Custer County embraced a section of southeastern Montana Territory that was almost as large as the state of Pennsylvania. You gents, Sam Chapman had gone on, got a fair to middling good idea where rustlers are hiding out. They'll call you back-stabbers and Judas's, or worse. But what you'll be doing will be a lot easer than taking that short walk out the west door to the gallows.

"Chapman's a tough old coot."

"Likes his whores, though."

"Gin." Kiley Glover took out a box of snuff. "It wouldn't take much to get the drop on Sam out there."

"Not since there's four of us."

"That's something we'll just have to keep in mind in case that old coot gets too bossy."

"What about sashaying back to check on them Cheyenne."

"Deal the damned cards, Chili. No way them dogeaters can chew them irons off . . . so deal."

The dark piercing eyes of Black Coyote went toward the stairway and the sound of laughter seeping down into the Basement Felony. One day these men were captives, as he was, and Hold-in-the-Breast and Running Boy. The next these same men wore badges and packed guns at their hips. He could not understand this. Nor could Black Coyote determine in his mind why the soldiers wanted to bring them here to Miles City.

Black Coyote had given up trying to break free of the handcuffs and irons snugged tight around his ankles. It would not be long, he sensed, before the white men would kill them. Last night he'd sung his final death song. Sharing his cell was Hole-in-the-Breast, somewhat younger, and bewildered by what was happening to him.

"Are you awake?"

"One cannot sleep in a place like this, Black Coyote. You said they will hang us."

"Soon . . . tomorrow perhaps . . ."

"We cannot escape this, nor rid ourselves of these irons. But if there was only some way to cheat them out of their sport."

"There is a way, my friend."

"Anything. I . . . I am not afraid to die . . . even

47

at my own hand."

"They did not take my belt strap." Black Coyote removed it from around his waist, then he secured one end to an iron bar in the aperture of the cell door. "See, Hole-in-the-Breast, both of us can move to the cell door."

A sort of soft, crazed laughter came from Hole-in-the-Breast. "Though our ankle irons are secured to these chains, we can raise up just enough to . . . to tie your belt around our necks. But do I have the courage to do this, Black Coyote? Inwardly I tremble."

"It is the way I have chosen."

"Then let me go first. While there is still some courage in me." He managed to crawl over, and with Black Coyote's help fasten the belt around his neck. He held there for a moment in an awkward sitting position, and with his eyes locked on Black Coyote. "There will be no reservation for Hole-in-the-Breast"

"Nor for Black Coyote."

Now he dropped to bring his full weight onto the belt wrapped around his neck. His body quivered even as it fought to drag air into his lungs. To end the death agonies of the other Cheyenne, Black Coyote pressed down on Hole-in-the-Breast's chest, and then it was over.

"You died bravely," intoned Black Coyote as he lifted the corpse and untied the strap from the neck of Hole-in-the-Breast. Lowering the body to the concrete floor, he adjusted the strap for his own hanging. Quickly he secured it around his neck as light suddenly splashed into the dark cell block. He stayed close to the door in a half-crouch when one of the men guarding them strayed past his cell. When

Deputy Marshal Chili Tugwell saw Running Boy glaring back at him, he snarled.

"Sure would like to get you in my gunsight." He unleathered his handgun and rasped its barrel along the cell bars. "Even hanging's too good for the likes of you." Then he strutted away and found the stairway.

Patiently the Cheyenne waited until he was certain the white man was gone. There were no regrets over what was about to happen in the mind of Black Coyote. Had not his own people sent him away in shame. Now to be hanged by those he hated. By taking his own life, Black Coyote knew he would bring honor to his name, for once his people found out what happened they would tell stories about him around the campfires.

"It is time."

The Northern Cheyenne threw his full weight upon the belt strap. For a moment pain exploded in his mind and trembled his yielding body. He could feel his hands bound by the handcuffs wanting to reach out and save him. But he resisted this in the last few moments left to him.

"Now, my brothers, you are with our father, Wakan-Tanka," came the sorrowing voice of Running Boy.

The remaining Cheyenne felt a deep loneliness overwhelm him. Softly, in an almost inaudible voice, he sang his own death song. After a while he rested. Running Boy, as had the others, would end this thing. But he would wait until first light pierced through the barred windows. This was a special time to him, for he called himself a morning person, or a son of the morning God.

Sometime later he could hear an outside door open, boots of those entering the courthouse echoing down to Running Boy, the muted voices of those standing guard. The night seemed to stretch on forever. Coming from the adjoining cell was the stench of death, but this did not trouble the Cheyenne. Barely into his twenties, he sent his thoughts away from this place and to a young maiden who favored him. About a month ago he had come across Moon Calf taking a bath in a secluded place along the river near the Cheyenne encampment. She'd enticed him through the willows and on a grassy bank they'd made love. Perhaps Moon Calf was with child. If so, he must die bravely, since Running Boy truly believed his spirit would return to his people.

When false dawn touched into his cell Running Boy removed the cords from his moccasins. Then he tied them together to form a hanging rope. To the metallic ringing of this chains he hunched over to the cell door and knotted one end of his rope to an iron bar. It would be around an hour, he knew before the jailor arrived, and Running Boy said gutturally in Cheyenne, "By then my spirit will have fled my body."

Though the cord was rather short, there was just enough of it to enable Running Boy to loop it around his muscular neck. Because of the heavy handcuffs, this was difficult work. When the knot was secure, Running Boy let his eyes lift to faint beams of sunlight just penetrating through a barred window, and he could even see a portion of blue beyond grayish clouds. Briefly, there arose in his breast a great yearning for what lay beyond Miles City. Only to have sadness film over his eyes.

"Black Coyote and Hole-in-the-Breast . . . I join you!"

Running Boy simple fell forward to have the joined cords from his mocassins cut deeply into his neck. He went to his death slowly, in agonizing pain, alone.

When jailer Ham Lauden showed up at the courthouse, it was to find those new deputy marshals hired by Sam Chapman sleeping, Mort Reiser in the marshal's big swivel chair and Joe McVay stretched out on a cot. In Lauden's opinion they hadn't been ideal prisoners, nor would they amount to much as lawmen.

Slamming his big ring of keys against the desk, Lauden rasped, "The honeymoon's over, you lazy buggers."

"Yeah . . . yeah . . ." Mort Reiser turned groggy eyes upon the jailer as he swung his boots down from the desk.

"I expect you've been keeping an eye on our prisoners?"

"What we're here for. Damn, I'm hungry."

"What you need, Reiser, is a hot bath. 'Cause you flat out stink."

Mort Reiser shaped a snaggly grin. "Don't bother my horse none."

"Nothing bothers a bugger like you," groused Ham Lauden. "McVay, hustle your lard butt over to Flanagan's Cafe and bring back some chow for our prisoners."

"What about breakfast for me and Mort?"

"When you're off duty. Come on, get a move on."

The dry weather of late had brought out that sinus problem Ham Lauden suffered from, meaning that he was in no mood to put up with former prisoners such as Reiser and McVay. He'd lost count of the times they'd been guests in the Basement Felony. Now they were starpackers. "Just what is this world coming to."

"When's the marshal gonna show?"

"When he gets good damned and ready, I reckon. Come on, Reiser, let's check out them Cheyenne."

The hardwood floor creaked under the weight of Ham Lauden moving toward the staircase. Followed by Mort Reiser, he went down the stairs and stopped so abruptly that Reiser stumbled into him. "What the hell's that smell?"

"Same old Cheyenne stink, Ham."

Ham Lauden's question was answered when he reached the cell and discovered the dead Black Coyote hanging by the closed door. At a glance he could tell the other Cheyenne were also dead. He stepped over to the next cell, glanced in, then he shouted at Reiser, "Fetch Sam Chapman on the double! And remember, not a word of this to anybody!"

Fifteen minutes later Marshal Sam Chapman, by habit a late sleeper, found himself viewing three dead Northern Cheyenne. Despite the voiced anger by Ham Lauden that it was sheer carelessness on the part of his deputies which brought about these killings, Sam realized this couldn't have been prevented. When a Cheyenne set his mind to something of this nature, neither another Indian or any white man could deter the end result. These Indians had sought death in a cool and deliberate manner, so unusual that it evoked in Sam Chapman admiration and a certain respect. In him too was a sad recollection of how the once great Cheyenne Nation had been virtually destroyed by the exodus of the white men out here. These Cheyenne simply could not understand what was happening to them or adjust to a new way of life on a reservation. All they'd known was the old ways. Perhaps, in death, their spirits had been liberated.

"I thought something was up."

Marshal Chapman glanced over to see the editor of the *Yellowstone Journal* peering down the staircase. Not too long ago Thompson R. McElrath had been a reporter for *The New York Times*. His newspaper had sent McElrath, then a reporter, out here to report on the Indian situation. Two months after arriving he'd started up the *Yellowstone Journal*. Except for the eastern suit, McElrath could have passed for a westerner with his lean frame and darkly tanned face. He'd taken to wearing cowboy boots and a cattleman's hat.

"They couldn't wait to be hung," Sam informed McElrath.

"Just being cooped up here was another way of dying to them," the editor said, upon coming over to peer in at Running Boy.

"Awright," Sam said regretfully, "Reiser, McVay, cover up the bodies while I go over and get the undertaker."

"I'll go with you, Sam."

Outside the courtroom, the editor and the marshal turned their eyes away from sunlight piercing through the scattering clouds and reflecting blindingly off a window pane. Upon receiving this appointment as a U.S. marshal, Sam had been more or less interrogated by McElrath. One of the subjects brought up by the editor was just how a man with no experience as a lawman could be given such a high position. To which Sam Chapman had responded that perhaps the Republicans were a desperate bunch. Later had come McElrath's talking to him about that girl of Annie Turner's getting murdered, that just maybe there was a connection to those other murders over at Big Timber and Bozeman.

"This is more or less still the raw frontier, T.R."

"Rawboned and sassy as hell," agreed McElrath. "Once I'd set eyes on the Yellowstone River flood basin and yonder mountains I knew there'd be no more back east for me. Every day seems to bring a new challenge."

"Just waking up is good enough for me."

Around a smile the editor said, "Doubt if you ever worried a drop in your life. But seriously, Sam, how do you think Judge Garth is going to react to what just happened?"

"You mean being cheated out of hanging them Cheyenne. He's a different breed, awright."

"I'd watch myself around him."

"Any particular reason?"

"All kinds of reasons, Sam. Garth troubles me. He's done harm to a lot of folks out here."

"I gather then, T.R., you're looking into his activities."

"Just between us I am. And I talked to Sheriff Pindale about the murder of that girl. Pindale figures it was some drifter."

"Like you just said, T.R., this is a rawboned and sassy place."

"Well, Sam, I've got a story to write."

After notifying the undertaker, Sam Chapman hurried back to the courthouse, and reached for his sixgun upon hearing shouts coming from the Basement Felony. He took the stairs two at a time, but pulled up short when he sighted Judge Harlan Garth forcing deputy marshals Reiser and McVay into a cell at gunpoint.

"I'm charging you men with not only killing those Cheyenne but jailbreak and impersonating an officer of the law!"

"Judge," Sam called out, "this isn't what it seems."

"So there you are, Chapman," Garth spat out. "I simply could not believe what your jailer told me . . . that these . . . these horse thieves are authorized to wear those badges."

"They are," Sam said curtly. "As for the Cheyenne, they took their own lives; happened last night."

Shoving his handgun into its holster, Judge Garth stalked toward Sam and the staircase. "Come on, Chapman, we have to talk."

Up in his spacious second-floor office, Judge Garth slammed his hat down on his desk and spun to face Sam Chapman, and with the marshal saying calmly, "Judge, you told me to put an advertisement in the newspaper. Which turned out to be a waste of time. So I had no choice but to make them hoss thieves my deputies."

"Once you leave Miles City, marshal, you'll be at their mercy. Besides, and this is the issue, Chapman, I have a reputation to maintain. The people of this territory will never honor my position as a federal judge when they see known outlaws wearing deputy marshal badges."

"A lot of folks out here were owlhooters or worse before they turned to honest labor. Kiley Glover and his bunch are no different. Just to make sure, I kept an ace in the hole. That being readers sent out on them just in case they revert back to their old professions. Which means they'll be hung if that happens. And what better way to catch hoss thieves, Judge Garth, than to send hoss thieves after them."

"You amaze me, Chapman. Out there you'll have to have eyes in the back of your head. But you've made your bed, I suppose. Now, Chapman, you sleep in it." The judge reached for some papers and thrust them at his new U.S. marshal. "Warrants that I want you to serve. You'll pull out of here first thing in the morning. Now get the hell out of my office."

Chapter Six

According to Kiley Glover some horse thieves generally hung out to the northwest along Great Porcupine Creek. To which Marshal Sam Chapman had responded, "Old friends of yours?"

"Just trying to justify your trust in us, is all. Nope, wouldn't call Randeen Schatz a friend."

"Who else rides with Schatz?"

"Sidekickin' him is a rascal named Bolanger . . . Eb Bolanger."

"That sounds like some kind of disease."

Glover paused in his shaping of a double-diamond-hitch long enough to chortle at Sam Chapman. Close by the other deputy marshals were checking their saddle rigging over. They were still inside Butler's Livery Stable, a newer frame building a block south of the courthouse. It had taken Sam an extra day to gather the provisions he wanted to take along, something which had displeased Judge Harlan A. Garth. The hostler, an old acquaintance of Sam's, hadn't been all that pleased at being rousted out well before sunup. But a silver dollar had quieted his loud mutterings. The gelding didn't take too kindly to being burdened with a pack-saddle, and it switched its tail at Kiley Glover.

"When you figure on being back?"

Sam Chapman glanced over at the hostler taking his ease in a wicker chair. "Don't rightly know, Clem."

"It better be during decent hours or them doors ain't opening."

"What you need is a snifter or two of corn mash."

"Got ulcers, doggonit."

"There's always the whores," said Joe McVay.

"Too old for that sinful stuff."

"Boot hill's just north of town then."

"I reckon we're ready," said Chapman, as he climbed into the saddle, to which the hostler rose stiffly and went to open the front double door.

The lawmen exited the livery stable to ride into pale sunlight just fetching over rooftops. As yet the wind hadn't started, something of a daily happening, and that when it warmed up more. They would have taken spare horses, but it was Sam's notion they could get fresh mounts at any one of the ranches they'd be passing by. Stowed on the pack horse was heavier clothing, to be utilized if they had to go into the mountains.

"Crowley's is just opening," Chili Tugwell informed them. "Maybe we could stop for a quick snorter."

Mort Reiser said, "You're still packing a hangover an' enough whiskey in you to last for a few days."

Around them the town was stirring, and a lot of business places showed lantern-light. Sam had expected to get out of Miles City before this, as he knew their leaving would arouse some curiosity. He wouldn't doubt but that a few outlaws were hanging around town. Catching them, he reckoned, was about the same as going fishing; there were always a lot of trout that got away. Off to his left Sam couldn't help noticing Editor McElrath peering out of an office window. Sure as the wind would pick up around midmorning, tomorrow's headline in the *Yellowstone Journal* would tell of federal lawmen heading out to arrest some rustlers. Could be this would drive up the price of railroad stock.

The horses heard it first, and they started acting skittish and swinging their heads to look down a sidestreet. Then Kiley Glover grinned as the packhorse he was leading kicked out with a hindleg, and with Glover blurting out, "Now who in tarnation would be tom-toming on a drum this time of day?"

Bong-Bong—Bong-Bong-Bong!

"Got kind of a religious beat to it?" wondered Joe McVay.

About a block upstreet the drummer, a bearded and suited gent, made his appearance, the drum sounding louder and causing Sam Chapman to rein up hard. Others emerged from the sidestreet, a mingling of men and women. They stepped out to form a human barricade across Main Street, and now Sam groaned when they broke out into song.

"Repent Thou Sinners . . . Repent. Give Thyselves To The Master."

Through his laughter Kiley Glover said, "They must mean you, Marshal Chapman."

Out of the buildings lining the street trickled a few people. While in Sam Chapman started building a little resentment. He'd heard rumors that some of the churches were protesting his appointing known outlaws as his deputies. As he started to rein down a convenient alleyway, a man shouted,

"Hold, Marshal Chapman." A man stepped past the drummer and toward the lawmen. In one hand he carried a large black bible, and now he raised it over his head. "I am Pastor Gordling of the Tabernacle of

God Church. You ride with sinners, Marshal Chapman. But it is not our intention to condemn these men . . . only to bring them salvation. Salvation!"

The drummer's arms flayed down at this drum. Bong-Bong — Bong-Bong-Bong!

"— Repent Thou Sinners . . . Repent! —"

"Come, you sinners, come hither on bended knee . . ."

"Let's ride," Sam muttered dryly as he sought the alleyway.

Just downstreet a gunhand presently employed by the Clearwater Ranch stepped away from the batwings when Marshal Chapman and his men swung down an alley. Bilo Mackley settled down at his table in J.B. Haskins Elegant Saloon and laid his eyes upon a high yellow known only as Cleo. They had just come down from her room when those lawmen had clattered by. Cleo had gotten to be one of his favorites, but as a lot of these women did, she'd probably pull out in a week or two and try her luck at another town on the circuit.

Mackley smiled as she poured chicory coffee into his tin cup. Under the chemise he could see the swelling of her full breasts. For a moment he was tempted to head upstairs to her bedroom. But the thought of what had brought Bilo Mackley to town held him at the table. He'd never killed a woman before. Could be that he would enjoy it. But why did Rye Garth want him to kill a whore from Mag Burns's stable? No use, he knew, trying to figure out the mind-bent of the man he worked for. About all Rye seemed to live for was his gambling and his whores. As for the dark forces that drove the owner of the Clearwater to kill, it just could be that when this was over Rye Garth would turn on him.

"Half the money now," muttered Bilo Mackley, "the rest when that whore's laid to rest."

"What did you say, honey?"

"Just ruminating, Cleo, on how cruel life can be."

And just for a moment her almond eyes widened to reveal a haunting look of despair and fear, then a quick smile pushed her inner thoughts away. "How long you gonna be in town?"

"Not sure. A day or two."

"I'll see you tonight?"

Bilo Mackley emptied his cup and stood up. What he needed at the moment was some fresh air, but mostly to be alone. "Could be."

Twenty minutes later he was aboard his horse and just about coming onto the brackish waters of the Yellowstone River. Pulling up under a cottonwood, he swung down and let the horse graze while taking out the makings and shaping a cigarette. The barest of winds came out of the northwest to caress his face, but Bilo Mackley seemed more aware of his vague image reflecting up from the river waters. That was how he viewed Rye Garth, a man with vague intentions, selfish yet so damned proud. It was Rye's pa getting him that ranch.

"Let's face it, Mackley, he scares you."

Inhaling tobacco smoke, the gunhand began debating over whether or not he'd overplayed his hand. Saying he would kill a woman, even a whore, was one thing. And, once it was over, could he live with himself, even though he had seven notches on his .45 Peacemaker. All I'll be doing, he reflected bitterly, will be pointing the finger of suspicion away from Rye Garth.

"And that sure as hell is gonna be worth more than a thousand dollars. Another thousand at least. Or Rye, his honor the judge will be coming after you again."

A long time ago an old friend of Sam Chapman's had told him to always watch his backside. Pondering over this as he eyed a red-tailed hawk soaring over the flood plain in its search for prey, the new U.S. marshal was having a few doubts about his present company. Covertly he'd been studying them as morning gave way to early afternoon. Thieves; no doubt about that. They certainly weren't any great shucks at being gunhands, though they carried enough armament. Sooner or later, if they hadn't done so by now, they'd hassle over their immediate future. Meaning any one of them might turn on him.

Up to now, he'd found out, none of them had killed a man. Back at the courthouse and in Sam's office, Kiley Glover had inquired about the new marshal's prowess with hand or long gun. Suddenly Sam Chapman's Smith & Wesson was out and nudging against Glover's nose, to have the disdain in the outlaw's eyes flicker into a grudging respect. Then Sam had flat-out lied, this is response to whether or not he'd killed anyone. At the time one or two had been better than a bragging half-dozen going down under Sam's gun. The truth is that Sam Chapman hadn't gunned down anyone. But he'd winged one or two during a poker session in an attempt to vacate the premises. And too, at the time, he hadn't thought that winging a man would carry too much weight with the likes of Kiley Glover and Joe McVay and the others. But just like in poker that little white lie was his ace in the hole.

"My rump's getting sore," groused Chili Tugwell. "An' my stomach's grumbling."

Mort Reiser snorted through his handlebar mustache. "Being waited on hand and foot back at that jail has really softened your gents up. Sam told us we'd noon when we got to Great Porcupine—that creek ain't more'n another mile or two."

"I humbly thank you for your support."

"A pleausre, Marshal Chapman."

"Kiley, how you coming with that pack horse?"

Kiley Glover nudged his horse into a trot to catch up with the others. Pulling alongside Sam, he said, "That gelding has worked out a lot of kinks . . . hasn't tried bucking for a spell now. Was me I wouldn't want to be burdened down with no backpack. By the way, Sam, just who are we going after this trip?"

"Those who've broken the law," responded Sam Chapman.

"You mean to tell me," spoke up Joe McVay, "that outlaws and hoss thieves out in these parts?"

Even Sam had to smile at this rejoinder. Up to now they hadn't talked much, just being content to let their horses settle into the trail and sort out silently anything that had been bothering them. All of them were capable horsemen, and even so, Marshal Chapman had set a cantering pace for most of the time. He felt there was no need to tire out the horses, for if they didn't encounter any outlaws today, there'd always be tomorrow and the days still to come.

Early summer had settled eagerly upon the Yellowstone Basin. It was a place of rolling prairie, delicately colored badlands, pine-covered mountains. Winding up and down ridges were the grass-grown scars of wagon trails with more scars out on the flats. Oftentimes a horseman would come across rifle pits and

63

rock shelters revealing where battles had been fought. One of the stories being told was that at the foot of a gnarled juniper near the crest of a short rocky ridge a soldier had left a handful of empty shells—mute evidence that a famous general did not tell the truth when he wrote about a fight. With the cessation of the Indian Wars some of the army posts stood empty, and buffalo grass still refused to grow where one of the most famous fur trading posts once stood. Now in the basin one found the Indian agencies and a scattering of ranches and the traditional cowtowns. Ancient belief has it that the Crow Indian, while trading in Mandan villages, described the basin, then known as the Elk River Basin, to a Minitari who rendered it Mi-tsi-a-da-zi to a French trader, and he in turn translated this to be Roche Jaune. All that is known with certainty is that from the time of the earliest traders on the Upper Missouri this river has been called La Roche Jaune—the river of the Yellow Rock.

Though Sam Chapman had seen a lot of prairieland in his wanderings, he had come to call the basin his personal stomping grounds. Although he was more intimately familiar with its towns, he could set out alone in these parts and ultimately find a place he'd been to before. Still, there were wild places a lot of white men had only heard about. And places that men like Kiley Glover could reveal to him. Mort Reiser's pointing out the mouth of Great Porcupine Creek brought them splashing across the shallow waters of the Yellowstone. With Reiser taking the lead, they loped northerly across the narrow flood plain, then let their horses labor up to prairieland an string out while following the creek. The creek still had plenty of water in it from spring runoff, and it was one of those sultry days.

Coming to a stand of elm trees, a word from Sam brought them closer to the creek. Swinging down, he said, "This'll be a cold camp."

"Reckon that won't hurt us none," said Kiley Glover. "But afterward, Mr. Reiser, I figure it's your turn to wetnurse this packhorse."

"Why not, I've been wetnursin' you long enough."

"Watch your mouth, Mr. Reiser," Glover said stiffly.

"Easy, boys," Sam cut in. "Maybe you'd better save some of your anger for those we're after." He rummaged around in one of the packs and come up with some dried beef and hardtack, which he passed out to his deputies. Then he eased down next to Chili Tugwell sitting on a fallen tree.

"You know, Sam, back a few years there wasn't all this much rustling. I suppose because of the Indians, and longhorns didn't sell for a heck of a lot." Kiley Glover uncorked his canteen and took a swig of water.

Sam Chapman said, "That's all changed since the ranchers started bringing in Oregon cattle. And Oregon horses."

Out of Texas to these parts had come both the longhorn and the Texas mustang. As the years passed, local ranchers began reaching out to Oregon for a more durable breed of both cattle and horses. Those who'd gone by wagon train out to Oregon had reached their destination with a cow or two as well as oxen, bulls and horses. Turned out to graze on virgin grass, they had multiplied rapidly. The root stock of Oregon's horse herd came from varying sources, the animals of the pioneers being bred to the fine animals the Hudson's Bay Company had brought in during the years when Great Britain was in possession of the country, and by excellent strains of Indian ponies bred by the Nez Perce. It was soon discovered by Montana ranchers that Oregon horses were more surefooted than the smaller Texas mustang, they were easier to handle and had the stamina to survive the bitter Montana winters. So for a time a lot of trail herds passed out of Oregon into places such as the Yellowstone Basin. And Sam knew that it was this demand for both Oregon horses and cattle that had seen a lot of rustlers drifting in from Wyoming and Colorado.

"That, gentlemen, is chiefly why we're out here."

"Why *you're* out here, Marshal Chapman," Mort Reiser said bitterly. "I'm here because I've got no other choice."

"The rest of you may feel as Reiser does," said Sam, "but as I recollect all of you were about half-a-step from being hung. Now north . . . up this creek someplace . . . are some rustlers. I don't care if they're friends of yours or not, not that you boys have too many you can trust or who'd loan you money. When you put on that badge you took an oath. An' so help me Hannah, you'll do your duty or answer to me."

"There's four of us!" said Mort Reiser.

"Mort, I don't reckon you're speakin' for me," Kiley Glover said. "The rest of you hear this. Sam, here, kept us from being hung. Yup, I know, he might have stacked the deck against us by sendin' out them readers . . . but what the hell, we owe him more'n one day's riding. We know how it feels to be on the dodge. Packing this badge sets a mite easier with me."

"What'll probably happen, Kiley," muttered Mort Reiser, "is someone punching a hole through that tinny little badge."

"You want to try it?"

"That's it," Sam said quickly, "let's move out. And just remember the both of you, don't let this sudden spate of bad feelings interfere with your sworn duty. I've a hunch that before too long we'll come across some thievin' wastrels. So keep your eyes peeled to that."

Chapter Seven

Miles City, christened Milestown at its birth, was the first settlement of any size in the Yellowstone Basin. It came into being in the fall of 1876 when Colonel Miles, becoming irritated at having a bunch of coffee-coolers underfoot, ordered them to move to the other side of a stake which he had ordered set a couple of miles east of the cantonment. A fragment of the trail between Fort Keogh and Bismark became Main Street, and on either side of this road the business section of the town sprang up. This included the parlor houses, notably among them Mag Burns's the 44 and a bordello run by the infamous Fanny French.

As had become a habit of long standing, Mag Burns took that four-block walk over to the Inter Ocean Hotel around midafternoon and was escorted to a table in its spacious dining room. Today she ordered a light repast, loin of beef, strawberry tarts and imported coffee. Most of her girls would be getting up about now, then readying themselves for tonight's business. But Mag's thoughts were on a brief chat she'd had yesterday with Sheriff Toby Pindale. Pindale had made vague comments about some kind of investigation he was conducting into the death of that harlot. What really had troubled Mag was the sheriff's refusal to offer any protection to her girls. This was one of the reasons why Mag Burns was seated at a front table giving her a view of Main Street, and she was also conscious of the curious glances of other diners.

Since coming here around five years ago, Mag had acquired bittersweet feelings about this town. It felt more like a typical border town than one stuck out in this wilderness. Past the wide window floated cowboys on their broncs, and an occasional buggy or dray wagon, and rough-looking characters, and locals she knew. The saloons never closed, and with the doors of most business places kept wide open during the hot summer months. But to Mag it was the fact she'd earned a certain respect.

"You are Mag Burns?"

She swung her head to the left and from under the dark blue bonnet a veil coming over her eyes looked up at a bulky man clad in an unobtrusive brown suit. The stranger had hard eyes in a blocky face, but she noted the way he'd doffed his western hat, and she murmured, "Please, Mr. O'Rourke, sit down."

Easing onto a chair across the table, Frank O'Rourke said quietly, "Tillie Marlowe sends her greetings, Mag."

"In her letter she spoke highly of you."

"Tillie's a grand lady."

"Coffee?"

"Please, ma'am."

"She told you what happened?"

"I know about the killing. And of the others over at Big Timber and Bozeman."

"So then, Mr. O'Rourke, you know my girls need

some kind of protection. I'll pay you a hundred dollars a week . . . and there'll be a room for you at the 44."

"That will be adequate. The law hereabouts . . ."

"Nothing will be done, I'm afraid."

Upon leaving the Inter Ocean Hotel with Frank O'Rourke, she directed him toward her place of business before turning the opposite way toward the Citizens Bank of Miles City. Coming to a street corner, a couple of loafers muttered low greetings to Mag Burns. Inwardly she smiled, for both of them were frequent visitors to her place, then with a pleasant nod she crossed the intersection and turned into the bank. At a teller window she removed from her large purse a leather pouch, only to be told by the teller that her presence was requested in the private office of bank president Charles Miller. There, Mag felt the door closing behind her as she placed concerned eyes upon the banker coming around his desk. In Charles Miller's eyes there was a certain luminosity and he was pallid of complexion.

"Mag, how long has it been . . . two months . . ."

"Charley Miller, you know it was last month at that ball out at Fort Keogh." Only a few intimate friends, and Mag Burns, ever called the banker by his nickname. It had been Charles Miller's support over the years that had seen her bordello come through some rough times. As he grasped her outstretched hand, Mag stepped forward and kissed him on the cheek. In her was this awful knowledge that he was dying, but she kept a smile in her eyes when she looked into his.

"Please, sit down, Mag."

He went behind his desk and dropped onto the big padded chair. "As you can see, I've lost some weight."

A good judge of character, Mag knew the banker to

be a man of considerable backbone, that her unexpected presence in his office could have nothing to do with his present illness. Probing into thoughts of the past, she realized that as a banker Charles Miller had to deal with both honest folks and those of questionable character. There were some people in these parts who shied away from dealing with the Citizens Bank simply because Judge Harlan A. Garth was one of its directors.

"Could you set up a meeting between myself and Marshal Chapman?"

The question took her by surprise. "With . . . Sam?"

"It must be done discretely. And . . . and soon, Mag."

"Sam's office is over at the courthouse, Charley?"

"No," he said sharply. "I . . . I can't tell you more than that."

"You've got it, Charley. Perhaps Sam can come to your house?"

"Yes, but at night. No one must know about this." He removed his handkerchief from his coat pocket and coughed into it. An apologetic smile etched itself across his thin face. "Smoked too darned much all these years, according to my doctor. Mag, you've been a dear friend. A lot of people, you know, the so-called upper crust, asked me why I would ever help someone like Mag Burns. I simply tell them you have a kind spirit. And you're an honest woman, Mag. I wish I had been more so."

They rose together, and she said, "Dammit, Charley, you get well."

"I shall try, Mag Burns."

"You know that Sam's out chasing after some rustlers."

"Heard that, Mag. And remember, nothing to anyone about this."

"Word of honor, Charley."

Gunhand Bilo Mackley had spent the last couple of days drifting in an out of saloons and gaming halls. Once he'd seen Judge Harlan A. Garth going into the Inter Ocean Hotel. This had only served to remind Mackley of why he was here. Never once had the gunhand thought that he'd need to build up his nerve to kill someone. Maybe he'd spent too much time the last few days thinking about Rye Garth. Last night Bilo Mackley had paid a visit to the 44. The unexpected presence of Frank O'Rourke, the new bouncer hired by Mag Burns, had set his killing plans back considerable.

"You in or out?"

The gunhand grimaced at the card player who'd just spoken before tossing in his cards and scooping up his remaining poker chips. He went over to the barkeep and cashed them in, then stood at the bar for a while drinking corn mash whiskey. He glanced up at the wall clock; a little after two on a weekday night in Miles City. Only those places cartering to the drinking and gaming crowd would be open. Pouring himself another shot of whiskey, the gunhand went over in his mind the layout of the 44. Though the back door was locked, some of the more shy customers entered the place that way, or left it. "Get on with it," Mackley finally told himself.

On his way out of the saloon he had to veer to keep from running into one of Sheriff Pindale's deputies, but with a muttered retort Mackley sidled upstreet. Then he passed down a narrower lane and in doing so, a bordello run by Fanny French. Some lights were still on, and in Mackley was a lingering temptation to head in for another drink and maybe a try at one of the whores. Instead, he strode on grimly to the livery stable and there set about saddling his bronc.

He brought his horse out the back way and walked it down a dark lane running to the north. At this time of night the few houses he passed weren't throwing out any light. Behind him a dog yowled, to be joined in by a couple of others. But the gunhand ignored this as he came around a shack to find himself about a half-block from the rear door of Mag Burns's bordello. Tied out back were two horses. Leaving his horse in the dark lee of the shack, Mackley went on until he came to a large cedar tree, where he crouched down and unsheathed his knife. He ran a thumb along the razor-sharp blade as the tinkling of piano music came faintly to him.

"Seems them whores are having themselves a grand old time," he said impatiently.

After a while there came the urge to have a smoke. As he started to unpocket the makings, the back door suddenly opened, and for a moment a suited man stood there talking back to someone inside the two-story building. The gunhand took this opportunity to hurry at a crouching run past the horses tied there and press himself against the back wall where he was partly screened by a large rose bush.

"The pleasure's been all mine, Irene."

"Ya'll hurry back soon, Mr. Pearson."

"Child, I'll do that." The man called Pearson swung away from the closing back door and moved clumsily toward one of the horses. Bilo Mackley darted forward just in time to keep the door from locking.

Mackley eased the door ajar and peered up the

74

back hallway, and then he slipped inside. The first inner door to his right was partly open, and from the light reflecting back down the hallway he could see that it was used as a storage room. Easing into the room, he sorted out what he was going to do next. It would all have been so simple if Mag Burns hadn't taken on that bouncer. As for the lower rooms lining the back hallway, they were used more for gambling and private parties, while the whores occupied the second floor. For a while the piano music had stopped, now it started again. And the gunhand was beginning to think that he'd made a mistake by coming here tonight, or of agreeing to do this killing for Rye Garth. The core of the matter was that Bilo Mackley wasn't a patient man. This was a failing that had gotten him into trouble more than once.

"Mr. O'Rourke," a woman sang out, "will you be so kind as to see if the back door is locked."

"What about Mr. Guthrie?"

"I believe Mr. Guthrie will be spending the night."

Bilo Mackley tightened his grip on the hunting knife when heavy footsteps resounded in the hallway. He held there until the bouncer had gone past to draw up the back door. Then the gunhand slipped out of the room. Quickly he brought an arm around to clamp a hand over Frank O'Rourke's mouth and plunged the blade deep into the man's back. He caught O'Rourke before he could crumple to the floor, and as quietly as possible he dragged the dying man into the storage room. He pulled the knife out and wiped the blood off on O'Rourke's brown suit coat. Coming out, he held there for a moment, flinched in alarm when a shadow passed across the large room beyond the hallway, mouthed a curse when he realized it had been a cat.

He padded on to the end of the hallway, and wheeled to his right and began slipping up the staircase. On the second floor, he prowled down the hallway to the two rooms at the rear of the building. Impulsively he opened the door to his left, then Mackley stared in at a woman sleeping alone in a feather bed, her black hair splayed out around her on the pillow, the heady scent of perfume tickling at his nostrils. Just briefly there arose in the gunhand a tingling of conscience. He could feel sweat popping out on his forehead as he deliberated over killing her or just finding his horse and heading out of Miles City.

"I don't kill her," he groaned, "that damned Rye Garth'll fix my clock for certain. Get it over with—quickly."

Entering, he closed the door and eased alongside the bed. The woman stirred and rolled onto her back. Mackley's hand shook as he picked up the spare pillow. He brought it down over the woman's face, used both hands to press down harder. He ignored the muffled scream, the flailing arms and legs, and then it was over. But not for Bilo Mackley as he discarded the pillow and groped for his sheathed knife. He made several slashes across the dead woman's face and down the throat and breasts, wicked cuts that spurted out blood.

"Enough," he blurted out, stumbling away from the bed to find the door and wrench it open. Still grasping the knife, he hurried down the hallway to the staircase and headed down it, only to pull up short when Mag Burns suddenly emerged from the darkened barroom. Without hesitating, he reversed his grip on the hunting knife and threw it at the startled woman.

"No!" she cried out.

Bilo Mackley saw her fall as he came off the staircase and ran down the hallway to wrench open the back door and disappear into the night.

Chapter Eight

One of the biggest mule deer Sam Chapman had ever seen exploded out of a thornberry thicket. In fact, Sam was so close he could see muscles rippling under the tawny hide, hear the faint bleat of alarm as the frightened animal bounded over shaly ground and vanished into a stand of firs.

"There goes supper," complained Kiley Glover.

"At least we found a living creature out here," Sam retorted.

About two hours ago Sam's deputies had brought him to an abandoned shack along the upper entrails of Great Porcupine Creek, the shack showing signs of recent use. Buried in a wooded gully along with the shack was a makeshift corral. In the shack they'd found discarded whiskey bottles and empty cans. But what had carried them out smiling and back to their horses was a deck of cards shredded by a disgruntled loser, to which Joe McVay had hooted that it must have been Eb Bolanger who'd done havoc to that deck. Still pricking at Sam's nostrils was a fetid stench left in that shack by a long line of occupants. The fresh trail they'd been following carried them away from the creek and southwesterly.

Around them twilight was spreading its wide skirts. While the tracks they were following oftentimes passed along an old game trail cutting through a ravine then back onto a tract of prairie. Sam's worry was that of losing the tracks in the uncertain haze of coming night. He'd voiced this to Glover, only to have the man respond with,

"I tell you, Sam, Randeen Schatz and Bolanger are heading for the Yellowstone. Them dozen hosses they've rustled will bring a fair price over at Benson's Landing."

"Benson's Landing? Seems to me it's located at the Great Bend of the Yellowstone."

"It is, Sam, and infested with rascals such as us."

"Just hope you rascals ain't thinkin' of traipsing over there for a class reunion."

"Imagine Marshal Chapman ever thinkin' us rascals ever went to school," cackled Chili Tugwell.

"A brain is a terrible thing to waste," sighed Sam. Last night they had camped south along Great Porcupine Creek, with Sam Chapman so jumpy he could only sleep in short spurts. But the night had passed uneventfully, and now with another night closing in, he didn't feel any easier. Mort Reiser worried him more than the others. The man seemed to have an acquired knack for complaining, while Sam was waiting for something to happen between Reiser and Kiley Glover. Whereas Chili Tugwell was just happy to tag along, taciturn Joe McVay had the coldest eyes Sam had ever seen in a man, kind of strange for one being so young. Coming from sparse backgrounds, he could understand how easy it had been for them to drift into a lawless life. Sam figured his hadn't been much better, or maybe, as the marshal of Dodge City had once told him, he'd been born under a lucky star. With night coming on, Sam Chapman knew he'd rather be looking up at one that having this star pinned to his chest, or better yet, safe and snug in some gaming casino.

"No more politics for this old wastrel."

Now his musings were disturbed by Kiley Glover veering over. "Randeen Schatz has a deep contempt for the law."

"That so?"

"Meaning, Sam, that he'll have a campfire."

"You're saying along the Yellowstone."

"Yup. 'Cause there's places flowing into the flood plain—ravines and such—rustlers use to corral their hosses. Or he could strike on for Pompey's Tower, camp thereabouts."

"You know, Mr. Glover, Benson's Landing is a long ways away."

"Oh, I doubt if Randeen Schatz has intentions of going that far. What he'll probably do, as others have done, rustlers that is, is sell those stolen hosses to the Ojeda gang."

"Carrying a warrant on Red Ojeda and others of his bunch."

"It'll be a sizable chore even gettin' close to them rustlers. Ojeda's got a lot of friends further west. Strange him operating this far east. Or maybe things are too hot for him thataway."

Farther west, or the country just mentioned by Kiley Glover, were the beginnings of the mountains. Rustlers oftentimes sold horses to miners in such places as Alder Gulch and Virginia, but the most infamous of these mining towns was Yellowstone City, a mining camp tucked up against the towering

81

Absarokas at the mouth of Emigrant Gulch. Recalling his quick passage through these towns, Sam Chapman knew them to be on the ragged edge of lawlessness. There were a lot of unmarked graves in that country, or sometimes a body was simply chucked into a convenient ravine or sinkhole. As for rustled horses and cattle, they were sold to eager miners without any questions being asked as to their pedigree, the brand they wore. So it was no wonder, Sam realized, that men like Red Ojeda and those they were tracking had gotten into the rustling game.

"Beats marshaling," he muttered, while straining to see in the gathering darkness. "You sure, Kiley, they'll beeline for the Yellowstone?"

"Want to bet a silver dollar on it—"

"Way my lucks' been lately, I'd lose. Okay, we'll press on."

Mort Reiser, who'd been riding off to Sam's left and on the other side of Chili Tugwell, said disgustedly, "Just a waste of time, dammit. I didn't like being forced into wearing this badge. Now we've got to ride all night just to catch up with Schatz and Eb Bolanger. It's becoming more clear in my mind that I just might vamoose for Wyoming or parts farther south and to hell with them readers out on me."

"That's an awful lot of words for someone dumb as you."

"Damn you, Glover, let's have it out right now!"

The harsh click when Sam thumbed back the hammer on his sidearm brought an abrupt halt to the argument and any ideas Glover and Reiser had of matching draws. Sam was tired, not being used to this hard riding and sleeping out on hard ground, and much like a father chiding his wayward children he lashed into them.

". . . so, dammit, I won't have any more of this tomfoolery. A fine thing if we kill ourselves before we catch, much less sight, a rustler. You wastrels are deputy U.S. marshals, so try actin' like it. I asked Kiley's advice as to the intentions of those we're after. But the decision to keep after them is mine. Come daylight they're bound to spot us closing in . . . meaning one or two of us could have our mangy hides ventilated. Now shut the hell up, the pack of you, and lets' ride. And you, McVay, take the point."

Vengefully night settled on the Yellowstone Basin as Sam Chapman brought his somewhat reluctant deputies at a canter across uneven stretches of prairie. They'd lost those tracks, but guided by vague starlight they kept angling toward the Yellowstone River. After a while a slender trace of curved light swung up over the horizon.

"See that," Sam remarked to break the long silence, "a quarter moon — what's more commonly known as a rustler's moon."

Chili Tugwell laughed. "When we rustled them cows, there sure as hell was a full moon out; reason we got caught."

"They wasn't cows and there was no moon that night," protested Kiley Glover. "Give me more credit than that." He glanced over at Mort Reiser expecting some snide remark, but strangely enough Reiser just sat glumly in the saddle watching his horse twitch its ears.

"That moon," Sam said, "should give us the edge. And I do believe we're coming onto the river."

Cautiously they rode along some high bluffs overlooking the flood plain until Joe McVay found a slashing cut which brought them down at a walk into scattered underbrush and stunted trees. Closing in on the river gleaming dully under a clear sky, Sam murmured.

"What do you think, Kiley, about them being west of us someplace?"

"Could be, since it's the direction they're intending to drive them stolen hosses. But knowing Randeen Schatz, there'll be a campfire."

"Hope we catch 'em soon," said Reiser. "Then what, find some cottonwood?"

"Bring 'em back for trial."

"Easier said than done, Marshal Chapman."

At this point the river was wide and still high but a dullish color, and on the north side of it they rode over exposed sand bars and gravelly ground which caused their horses to make a crunching sound. Only when they came around a wide bend in the river did Joe McVay, still riding out front, hold up an arm as he reined up. Pulling alongside McVay, they soon detected the faint glimmer of light on the same side of the river and under a sheer bluff below which there was a scattering of trees.

Kiley Glover said, "Camped up there before, Sam. Just beyond that bluff there's a sort of deadend gully; just deep enough to make a handy corral."

Grunting something in reply, Sam twisted in the saddle and fumbled his field glass out of a saddlebag. Through it he scanned the riverbank ahead, and then he said, "Seems there's someone down along the water's edge; could be trying his hand at fishing. You said you rode with them before?"

"Not when they was rustling," responded Glover. "But we parded around some, Randeen and Eb and me. So?"

"So I want you to take Tugwell with you. Just mosey on up there and introduce yourselves . . . real pleasant like."

"That Schatz has a reputation of slinging lead first and introducing hisself afterwards," Kiley Glover protested.

"Along with that badge you hombres are drawing federal pay. And that includes all expenses if a doctor is needed — by them or you."

"Well, that's sure different, Sam," Glover muttered. "Come on, Chili, we've got to start earning our federal pay."

A low word from Sam brought the others away from the exposed bank and back into sparse underbrush where they ghosted after Glover and Tugwell. By Sam's estimate they were about a half-mile from that campsite and time to split up and move in cautiously. One concern was of the horses alerting the rustlers to their presence.

"Joe," he said, "think you can find a way up onto that bluff?"

"Shouldn't be too hard."

"By the way, just how well did Kiley know those rustlers?"

"Well enough to get cheated at cards by them."

"Kissing cousins, uh."

"Don't worry, Sam, Kiley won't pull a doublecross by trying to warn them." Spinning his horse around, Joe McVay passed under a cottonwood and found some screening underbrush.

"That leaves me and you, Mr. Reiser. You feel up to this?"

"Up to dying," snapped Mort Reiser. "Not hardly."

"Me either. Which is why, Mr. Reiser, I don't want you lingering around my backside. We'll work our way in side by side so's I can eyeball you and that dun you're riding."

"I could have cut out last night, Chapman, and be hell and gone from all of this."

"Well, why didn't you?"

"Reasons."

"Expect you got lots of them, awright."

Up along the riverbank about a quarter of a mile the first twinges of unease were nudging at the minds of Kiley Glover and his cohort, Chili Tugwell. They had brought their horses to a slow walk and now drew them up and eyed one another. Vaguely they could make out someone casting a fishing line into the sluggish waters, and where they sat in the saddle the only cover was a stunted pine and a fat frog croaking almost underhoof. And without Marshal Chapman's close presence it came to them, a second or two apart, that a tug at their reins would bring them across the river and seeking a more healthy line of work. Spreading across their faces was indecision.

"What we gonna do, Kiley?"

"The night's young—same's us."

Confusion crept into the other's eyes.

"What I mean, Chili, is that maybe both of us won't be getting any older. That's a hard notion to think on."

"Always figured I'd go down in a blazeout."

"But, Chili, I know for gospel fact you ain't never been with a woman before. Now ain't that true?"

The portion of moon had risen more to add an uncertain glow to the stars and the land below.

Distantly the yip-yapping of a coyote sent their horses to tugging at their bits along with forcing the undecided minds of the young deputies into some kind of decision.

"Honest work would be more in the line of shoveling horse turds out of some livery stable."

"That for a stinkin' fact, Chili."

"I like this badge . . . bein' considered of some importance. Just bein' able to hold my head up proudlike, Kiley."

"We'll see how high you hold your balding noggin after I sing out to announce our unworthy presence." Kiley Glover raised himself in the saddle and drew night air into his lungs. Then he shouted, "Hello the camp!"

Both of them couldn't help noticing how the fisherman suddenly vacated the river bank and sought deep shelter.

"This is Kiley Glover! Been told Red Ojeda was hereabouts!" He reined on, followed by Chili Tugwell.

Closer, they could see embers sparking away from a large campfire, and then someone called out from a dark copse of trees, "Kiley Glover you say! Just where was the last time we saw one another?"

Glover pulled up sharply and yelled back, "At Frenchy's trading post over at Ridgeway. That you, Randeen?"

"What cards did I hold in that last hand?"

"Your three aces whomped my pair of nines."

"Ride on in, but slowly . . ."

They brought their horses around a cottonwood and away from the river about ten rods and dismounted close to the campfire. Both of them had taken the precaution of removing their badges, and even so, one false move on their parts could see these rustlers pumping leadén slugs into them. Kiley Glover could make out the dim forms of horses back in a gully, closer, those ridden by the rustlers. They smiled at Eb Bolanger stepping out from behind a rockpile, then Randeen Schatz came in from the other direction, the rustler saying happily,

"Imagine, Kiley, a-seeing you all the way out here. It sure boggles the mind, it does."

"Sometimes it's a small world, Randeen. Howdy, Eb."

"Howdy yourself," Eb Bolanger said sullenly.

"Got coffee and prairie strawberries warming over the fire. Just tie up them hosses. But sorry to say we done run out of corn liquor." Randeen Schatz's eyes rolled suggestively. "Don't suppose you're packin' any along?" He set his rifle down on his saddle and hitched conceitedly at his gunbelt.

"Should have brought some," said Glover, "as we only seemed to get along when you was a couple of sheets under the wind, Randeen."

"What the hell's that supposed to mean?" Then the rustler, and Eb Bolanger, were gaping at the barrel of Kiley Glover's sixgun covering both of them. "You gone loco, Glover?"

As Chili Tugwell pulled his handgun and stepped behind the pair of rustlers, Glover said, "Back at Frenchy's you was using a hold card; a fifth ace hidden in your sleeve. I was just sober enough to catch that. It boils down to your cheatin' me out of twenty dollars gainfully earned."

"You never did an honest day's work in your life, Kiley."

"Maybe so, Randeen, but it don't make a no difference now." Unbuttoning a shirt pocket, Kiley Glover fished out the lawman's badge and held it so that the silvery badge shone dully by the flickering campfire. "Chili's a-wearin' one too, boys."

"You worthless scum . . . lawmen?"

"You stole 'em!" lashed out Eb Bolanger.

"That's it," said Schatz, "this is just some kind of con game. Well, you ain't gonna take them hosses we rustled." His right hand stole toward the holstered .45 Peacemaker.

A derisive smile on his face, Glover said, "Makes no difference if I gun you down out here, Randeen, or take you back to stand trial. Look about, boys, there's others with us."

"That's right," Marshal Sam Chapman responded as he moved closer to the campfire, "I'll swear to their bonafides as U.S. marshals. Divest them of their sidearms, Chili. That coffee I smell?"

"Sure, you stinkin' lawmen, help yourselves to our vittles."

"Intend doing that, Mr. Schatz." Sam Chapman pulled Schatz's wrists together and put on a pair of handcuffs. "Cold steel always gave me the chill. Which reminds me, it's gettin' kind of chilly out."

"But don't worry," cut in Kiley Glover, "where you two are a-going it gets tarnable hot."

"Damn your smartmouth, Kiley!" muttered Eb Bolanger. "Should have gunned you down right off."

Under the watchful eyes of Chapman their prisoners were roped sitting to limber pines a short distance away from the campfire. To Sam they were a couple of no-accounts, smalltime rustlers eking a few dollars out of the horses they would eventually sell to unscrupulous horse traders or to men such as Red Ojeda. There were a lot of Randeen Schatz's lurking in the Yellowstone Basin. Only because they'd been acquainted with Kiley Glover had they been captured without gunplay. Now Sam figured his next move was to find out from Randeen Schatz where he'd planned to rendezvous with the Ojeda gang. Grimacing at the sour taste of the coffee, Sam emptied his tin cup on the ground and rose. He replaced the cup in a saddlebag and took out his pocket knife as he ambled over to gaze down at Randeen Schatz.

"Comfortable?"

"Go to hell, Chapman!"

Around a smile Sam cut away a small branch, and squatting down, whittled away until he'd fashioned a toothpick. All the while the rustler had been glaring at him, as had Eb Bolanger tied to a neighboring pine. "So, you wastrels, a lot of folks consider me a patient man. But tonight I feel out of sorts 'cause of all this riding I've done lately. So I'll ask you wastrels this question but one time—where were you taking them stolen hosses?"

Randeen Schatz just sat there stonyfaced, what he felt about Marshal Chapman dancing about in his sullen eyes. Close by, Eb Bolanger snickered, and then he said, "What hosses, marshal?"

Shrugging, Sam kept on picking away at his teeth. Now the moon was hanging more over the flood basin to throw pale slivers of yellowish light down upon the murmuring river. Occasionally there'd be the eerie call of a loon and once a roaming coyote yip-yapped its forlorn call as it sought another of its kind. But their horses seemed contented now that the saddles had been removed, though Kiley Glover's grulla would whicker and stamp about at times in its eagerness to join those rustled horses waiting out the night in that makeshift corral. This was a night, Sam mused, to be spent at some saloon instead of out here roughing it. And it could be a night for a hanging or two.

"I know you wastrels was figuring on selling them hosses to Red Ojeda. 'Cause that's about as far as you got this business figured out. Come sunup you boy's don't come up with some answers, that high branch on yonder cottonwood'll have a hanging rope slung over it. Sweet dreams, boys."

Chapter Nine

"There, that does it." Whereupon Kiley Glover handed Marshal Chapman one of the riatas on which he'd formed hangman's nooses.

Snaking the riata over a high limb on a cotton-wood, Sam reached for the noose dangling about eye level. To the east along the floodplain a thatch of thin gray clouds reflected morning sunlight. Across the shadow-strewn river and upstream some mule deer had come out to drink. There was no wind. Upon arising just before sunup, Kiley Glover had mentioned that it was a good day for a hanging, which had provoked from Randeen Schatz a tirade of cussed words as to Glover's pedigree and where his companions could go. In a flat aside, Sam Chapman had told the rustler to curb his unruly tongue.

Sam's stomach was still grumbling in protest from a breakfast of side pork and burned sourdough biscuits as he motioned for Randeen Schatz's horse to be brought over; a burp interrupted his thoughts on the hanging about to take place under a clearing sky. Last night he'd eye-measured the girth of Schatz's thickset neck much as a tailor had once measured him for a suit in far-away Denver. That hand-tailored dark blue suit had passed the muster along with catching the eye of his third and last wife. Though somewhat worn, that irresponsible suit had been burned with Sam Chapman vowing on a worn deck of cards never to wear that particular attire again. And he never had.

After Chili Tugwell walked the bronc under the cottonwood and stood there gripping the reins, Sam widened the noose while gazing coldly up at rustler Schatz. The plan he'd concocted with his deputies was for the horse to be slowly walked out from under the dangling Randeen Schatz, this to let the rustler, and Eb Bolanger, know that death was imminent unless one or both of them gave up all this cursing and came forth with some honest words and information. Sam knew this was asking a helluva lot. There was even the possibility that Schatz could choke to death or have his neck broken. But as far as Sam was concerned, and with his limited knowledge of the law, the power conferred on him as a U.S. marshal spoke louder than lawbooks or thieving lawyers. That last was a thought he reveled in; another raucous burp affirmed his bold opinion.

He could see it on Randeen Schatz's face that the man didn't expect to be hung by a U.S. marshal. And sneering back, Sam reached up and grabbed a hunk of sandy hair. He forced Schatz's head down, then he looped the noose around the man's neck and drew it tight.

"Last chance, Mr. Schatz."

"Last chance for what, damn you?"

"Along with that dirty mouth, you're awful stupid. Ojeda don't care what happens to you, or Eb

94

Bolanger. He'll just get hosses from other rustlers."

"Even if I might know something, Chapman, I ain't spilling the beans. I just might get a reputation like Kiley Glover and the rest of his turncoats."

"A bad rep's better than skydancing."

"Bullcrap—as a U.S. marshal it's your duty to bring me back to stand trial."

"There's such a thing as turning state's evidence. Meaning that you'll only have a long prison sentence eyeballing you. That is, if you was to cooperate."

"I ain't seen a lawman yet I can trust."

"That your last word on this?"

"That, and get this damned rope off my neck and let's make tracks for Miles City."

"You're going farther than that," Sam said gruffly as he turned to the cottonwood and looped the rope around it the one time. Drawing the slack out of the rope, he gave it a hard tug just to watch the rustler squirm and gasp out in pain and sudden fear. Then at a nod from Sam, Chili Tugwell walked the horse out from under its rider. Right off, the rustler's eyes seemed to bulge out of their sockets and he was still kicking and fighting for life when Sam yelled at his companion, "Okay, Eb Bolanger, you're gonna be next unless you tell me where you and Randeen were taking those horses!"

Eb Bolanger, being held alongside his horse by Joe McVay and Mort Reiser, kept his terrified eyes fixed on the man he'd been riding with. His face was the color of smoke issuing from the campfire, and then Bolanger cried out, "We was to meet with Ojeda near the Great Bend of the Yellowstone . . . I swear we was . . ."

Sam Chapman simply let go of the rope to have Schatz take that short drop to the ground. For a while the rustler didn't move, and Sam had the notion he could have breathed his last. Then Randeen Schatz began throwing out reedy gusts of air and stirring a little.

Laughing, Glover muttered, "That was some show, Marshal Chapman."

Around a hard smile Sam replied, "Not too long ago I was gonna oblige you the same way. Soon's Schatz gets his color back we'll ride."

"After Red Ojeda?"

"Too far a piece, what with us having these prisoners and those stolen hosses. Chili and Reiser, I want you boys to return those Bar D hosses. I expect you know where the Bar D is located."

"Can do," responded Chili Tugwell.

"Then you boys make tracks for Miles City."

"Is that where we're going?" said a dejected Kiley Glover.

"Right now, yup." Along with getting rid of these prisoners there was in Sam Chapman a strong and sudden desire to get reacquainted with Mag Burns as well as some corn whiskey. "Okay, boys, get them wastrels aboard their broncs. And us capturing them should sure-enough tickle Judge Harlan A. Garth's hanging bone."

For about the last hour Chili Tugwell's daydreaming thoughts had seen him become a U.S. marshal same as Sam Chapman. The badge pinned to his chest, the scrawny and thin-lipped deputy was beginning to realize, was a far more powerful aphrodisiac than rustling or breaking and entering. Tugwell could visualize himself taking out after Red Ojeda or other famous owlhooters. His draw would be swift and deadly.

Since noon Tugwell and Mort Reiser had been bringing the stolen horses due north. They hadn't spoken, not that Chili Tugwell hadn't in mind to do so, but simply because Reiser seemed to be in one of his foul moods again. A long line of trees cropping up when they rode over an elevation told Tugwell they were closing on the upper reaches of Great Porcupine Creek, and a distant butte also revealed their exact location. Farther to the northwest was the Judith Basin, a fertile reach of prairieland above the Musselshell River. While to the east of that lay the Bar D spread. Even though Tugwell was wearing his badge pinned to his vest, just hazing these rustled horses along made him nervous.

"It would be just our luck, Mort, to run into some Bar D hands."

"Perhaps we won't have to go that far."

"Something troubling you?"

Mort Reiser edged his cantering horse closer to Tugwell's. "These broncs would bring a fine price over at Benson's Landing. I say we take them over there and find out."

"You crazy, Mort. We's lawmen now."

"Hellfire, Chili, we're just out here doing Marshal Chapman's dirty work. So far we've been lucky. Next rustlers we encounter won't be so accommodating. All I'm saying is I ain't dying for no deputy's pay . . . not me, dammit."

"Maybe I kind of like it."

"Maybe you do, Chili. Which is just plumb loco. Figure it out, Chapman practically handed us these rustled hosses. We haze them over to Benson's Landing—get some handsome pay for a-doing it—then backtrack to Miles City. Act as if nothing happened."

"Nope," Tugwell said firmly, "it would be goin' against the grain. I's a lawman now, Mort, plan to keep it that way."

"Then you've let that damned badge twist your mind around." Mort Reiser swore as Tugwell spurred ahead and brought some of the horses back into the line of travel. "You're turkey dumb." Frustration and anger lidding his eyes, Reiser pulled out his Winchester, levered it, shouldered the weapon in and shot Chili Tugwell in the back.

The horses broke away as Tugwell flopped to the ground, and with Reiser riding up and sending a killing slug into the man's head. It took Reiser about a half hour to catch Tugwell's bronc and round up the rustled horses. Then he spurred his horse and the others into a westward course of travel.

They found Miles City as they'd left it, windy, maybe a trifle louder as dusk spread over the basin. Only this time there was no sermonizing preacher waiting to waylay them. Behind the courthouse the lawmen got down wearily from their saddles. Untying the blue bandanna from around his neck, Sam used it to wipe the dust from his face. No light poured out of the Basement Felony, and he knew jailer Lauden had left for the day. But he'd bet plenty that Judge Garth was still lingering in his office.

"Joe," why don't you tend to the horses. Me and Kiley'll deposit these prisoners in a cell."

"Yeah, Joe," said Glover, "I'll join you over at the Second National Saloon for some cold beer." He helped Eb Bolanger down from the bronc and went after Sam, herding the other rustler through the narrow back door and down a dark staircase to the basement cells.

"I need a sawbones," whined Randeen Schatz as he stumbled into a cell and sat down on a hard bunk. "My neck hurts somethin' fierce. Dammit, Chapman, you had no right to do that."

"You had no right to rustle them hosses. Least this way you'll be carrying that rope brand around for the rest of your miserable life, which just might end shortly. I'll see chow's sent over. So rest easy, gents."

"If you don't mind, Sam," said Glover as they came up the staircase by Sam's first-floor office.

"Get some cold beer, Kiley. Wish I could join you . . ."

"When you figure on pulling out again?"

"That'll be up to the judge, I reckon." In his office, Sam slumped down behind the desk, and from a lower drawer lifted out a bottle of Carstair's Best. He savored that first mouthful, and a second. But a scowl lifted his eyes when footsteps echoed into his office, and somewhat reluctantly he put the bottle away.

"I saw you come in Marshal Chapman."

"That so, Judge Garth."

"Who did you bring in?" he asked around a

pleasant smile.

"Rustlers—Schatz and Bolanger." To Sam Chapman it seemed out of place that the judge would actually smile. Maybe Garth had it in mind to fire him as a U.S. marshal. He sure wouldn't argue about it.

"There has been another killing here, marshal. A woman; some harlot employed by Mag Burns. But this time we know who did the killing . . . and I'm positive it is the same man who killed those other girls. Yes"—again the judge flashed a pleased smile—"it is most certainly the same man. Well, I'll see you in the morning, Chapman."

With the abrupt departure of Judge Garth, the hand of Marshal Chapman removed that whiskey bottle again. Why would the judge take such a keen interest in these killings? Perhaps too much so. Or perhaps Garth just liked to see men hanging outside his courthouse. Savoring the whiskey, Sam couldn't help feeling it was more than that.

"What'll the judge do if I get gunned down? Bust his guts laughing. Or declare a holiday out here. Garth's sure enough got a weird sense of humor."

Then he thought about Mag Burns and of one of her girls getting killed and probably buried by now. For a fact she'd need a shoulder to cry on. And just how did he feel about Mag, other than the 44 was a nice place to hang out.

"Head over there and find out, Chapman."

"You mean the judge didn't tell you?"

"All Judge Garth said was that he knows who the murderer is."

"Nothing about Mag, Sam?"

"You mean she's . . ."

"No," broke in Cowboy Annie, one of the courtesans working here at the 44, "Mag was knifed . . . but she'll be okay. She's up in her bedroom, and believe me, Sam, just as bossy as ever."

"Who got killed?"

"A new girl, Camille something or other. We gave her a proper burial."

With a smile for the girl, Sam bypassed the barroom and found the staircase. The door leading into Mag Burns's bedroom was open, but still he rapped, and at her muted response crossed the threshold. To him she looked fetchingly beautiful in a lacy blue nightgown. A bandage covered Mag's left shoulder. Though her eyes had responded with a smile, he could see the pain in them mingled with a kind of sadness that told him Mag Burns was also grieving for the girl, Camille.

Chidingly she said, "You took your own sweet time about getting back."

"Tarnable law business. Just what did happen, Mag?" He eased down on the edge of the wide bed, and leaning toward her, they kissed gently, a sort of lingering kiss that revealed how they felt about one another.

"Told both the sheriff and Judge Garth all I knew, which wasn't much. It happened as we were closing, five days ago now. Saw this gent traipsing kind of funny down the staircase. Next thing I know there's a knife sticking out of my shoulder. Then I passed out. Later I found out the new bouncer I'd hired had been killed . . . along with Camille."

"Did you get a good look at the killer?"

"A brief one. But I've seen him before; only thing is trying to place just where and when."

"Here, at your place?"

"Could be, Sam, could be. Strange, but when I described what the man looked like to Judge Garth, the judge had this strange look."

"Wouldn't be a smile would it?"

"No, more like he knew the killer. Like he was relieved about something. You know, like when the doctor tells you you don't have smallpox."

"The judge does have his strange ways. You'll be awright?" He reached for her hand.

"Come on, Sam, you know they've been trying to do away with us old warhorses for a long time. I'll be up and around in no time. But there is something else. Charley Miller is hankering to see you."

"Banker Miller? Never has extended me a line of credit or given me a loan. Matter of fact, Mag, last time I traipsed into his bank I was asked to leave by the back door; it's a wonder that reformin' preacher wasn't there to meet me so's to give me salvation. Don't make no sense, Mag?"

"Sam, it does when I tell you that Charley Miller is dying."

"That old buffer goin' under?"

"Charley's awright, as you say. Just different. And he's the reason I still have this place. He swore me to secrecy as to his health and wanting to see you."

"Would this be confession time? If so, maybe I'd better bring that preacher fella along."

"Perhaps you could go over to Charley's house tonight, Sam, see what this is all about."

"And leave you all alone in this featherbed."

"Don't you get any ideas, Marshal Chapman."

102

Her throaty laughter filled the bedroom, and it brought a relieved smile to Sam's face.

"Best I leave then, a-fore certain things happen. I'll go see Charley Miller, at your behest. Come tomorrow though, this old warhorse is gonna get a few things straightened out with his honor, the elusive Harlan A. Garth."

Chapter Ten

Many a time Bilo Mackley had bypassed lowslung Calumet Butte on his way down to the Clearwater Ranch. All he'd ever given that piece of high land and the rugged gulches and wooded ravines spreading out below it had been a casual glance at best. It had simply been there, same as had been grazing cattle and pronghorns keeping a respectful distance out on the long reaches of prairie.

In the days after the killing of that whore that butte had become a hiding place for the gunhand. Two days to be exact. For Bilo Mackley was not the kind to avoid a gunfight. Only this time it would be different, he knew with a fatalistic certainty, him by his lonesome against Rye Garth's hired guns.

The gunhand emptied the little water remaining in his canteen over the small campfire. His saddled horse waited patiently under the branches of a buckthorn tree. Common sense told Mackley to be satisfied with the money Rye Garth had given him and head into new territory. But common sense wasn't the coin of exchange for a man on the dodge. Mag Burns. He knew his knife had struck home, but she could still be alive, and able to identify him. Which to Bilo Mackley meant that he would be blamed for those killings committed by Rye.

"Let's face it, you were suckered on this one."

He went over and began checking the saddle rigging, and there he suddenly remembered a conversation he'd overheard between Rye and Judge Garth. Yes, about a month and a half ago out at the ranch. Mostly it had been the judge railing at his son. Jogging at his memory were such words as Chicago and some murders committed there . . . now it's happening out here . . . Rye protesting his innocence.

Saddlebound, the gunhand brought his rangy gray at a slow walk down the sloping game trail curling around rocks and pines and toward the main road passing on this side of the Tongue River. As he set the gray into a canter, Mackley knew he should probably head the other way, meaning the sanctuary of those settlements in the mountains. But in Bilo Mackley was this stubborn bent of mind that oftentimes had gotten him into trouble.

"Rye Garth owes me five hundred dollars, and I aim to collect it."

But he knew it was more than the money. Before coming up here to Montana there'd been the five years Bilo Mackley had served at the Oklahoma territorial prison, this for getting caught after robbing the Western Bank of Texola. He would have gotten a longer sentence, but the deal worked out with that district judge was him confessing to some of the other crimes he'd committed and fessing up to some he hadn't just to clear the judge's slate. Afterward, the lure of easy money as he worked his way up north had seen him rob a stagecoach and a

Colorado bank. Despite this, there were no readers out on him.

"Not up until now . . . until I listened to that damned Rye Garth."

Coming onto the main road, Bilo Mackley veered to the south. The moon, as it had been for about a week, was just a slice of yellow but throwing out enough glare so that he could keep to the road. At this time of night about all those using it would be cowhands either making that long ride to Miles City or heading back to ranches. His fear was of encountering someone from the Clearwater Ranch. He could strike out cross-country, but that was a longer route, and somewhat hazardous at night.

"Don't care how long it takes me to get there . . . midnight or after. I know Rye'll be there. Then what, gun him down? Do that and I'll sure as hell announce my presence to his men. Probably just get my money and make tracks out of there."

Gunhand Art Waddell yawned and tossed in his cards. "Seems you beat me again, Rye. Awful late — suppose we should call it a night."

"What else is there to do out here," said Ray Sundby as he swept the deck of cards together and began shuffling them. "Have some more whiskey, Art."

On Rye Garth's face was a worried frown as he drummed his fingers on the table. What was keeping Bilo Mackley? It could be Mackley hadn't ridden up to Miles City but cut out west someplace. Then, a couple of days ago, who'd showed up here at the Clearwater but Sheriff Toby Pindale to confer privately with segundo Phil Brady, and with Pindale striking right back to Miles City. This had set Rye to thinking, that the only reason the sheriff had come out here was by order of Judge Garth. Could it be that Mackley had gone to Miles City after all . . . killed some whore . . . and was hiding out or, as he'd already surmised, pulled out.

"Tomorrow, we're making tracks for Miles City."

"Since it's almost tomorrow now, Rye, why bother hittin' the sack?"

"Yup," grunted Sundby, "This whiskey ain't all that bad an' I'm about breakin' even in this game."

"Suppose I could take some more of your ill-gained money," said Rye. "But not on an empty stomach; Waddell, go roust the cook whilst I answer the call of nature."

All three of them rose, Art Sundby to move over to the fireplace and drop on another hunk of wood, Rye Garth following the other gunhand down a wide hallway in the spacious ranchhouse and come out onto the back porch, where Waddell continued on toward the log cabin used by the cook, a Chinaman named Li Wong and his wife and kids. Coming off the porch, Rye Garth sought the deeper shadows along the side of house. But what the rancher didn't expect to happen was to have his arms pinioned and the cutting edge of a knife pressed against his throat.

"You so much as spit, Rye, and I'll end your miserable life," hissed Bilo Mackley. "Here's the way of it. We're going into your office where you'll open that big black safe and pay me the rest of my money . . . and just maybe a few more dinero to tide me over. Come on, ease along now."

Mackley brought the rancher farther along the wall to a side door. They stepped into a short hallway, then he forced Rye Garth into a small room reeking of tobacco smoke. Unleathering his sidearm, Mackley shoved the rancher toward the safe reposing in a corner. "Get to it."

"What . . ."

"You speak any louder than that, Garth, and to hell with your money as I'll gun you down."

Rye Garth whispered hoarsely as he knelt down by the safe and fumbled for the dial, "What the hell you acting this way for, Bilo? I gave you half of the money, the rest after . . ."

". . . I do your dirty work. I killed one of Mag Burns's whores, and some gent she had there as a bouncer. But she saw me, Mag did, which means every lawman in the territory will be lookin' for me. That's right—just ease that safe open—and all of it, Rye, damn you." From the desk he picked up a leather pouch and tossed it over to the rancher.

"Bilo, it don't have to be this way," said Rye as he passed the leather pouch to the gunhand.

With a muttered curse Bilo Mackley slammed the barrel of his gun down on the rancher's head, and as Garth sagged to the floor, someone called out, "Hey, Rye, wat'cha doing in there?"

Quickly Mackley sprang toward the window and opened it, and as the office door began opening, he triggered a shot in that direction before scrambling through the window and dropping heavily to the ground. He broke toward his horse tethered behind the hip-roofed barn. In the saddle, he sought the few elm trees to the west. Afterward, the gunhand held his bronc at an easy gallop as he worked his way around scattered bunches of cattle. When he came to rougher country, Mackley slowed to a canter. They'd be after him, he knew, not the working hands but just Rye and those hired guns. How long until sunup, two hours at most. Even now night was loosing its hold on the land. He came to a creek meandering through a wooded ravine to ride his bronc along the muddy bank instead of trying to hide his tracks in the shallow water. After a while the ravine bent to the north, and it was here that Bilo Mackley broke through underbrush and urged his mount up to a jumbled pile of boulders, behind which he dismounted. With his Winchester in hand, he settled down among the rocks. They'd been drinking, and probably passing the night by playing cards, and after what he'd done to Rye Garth, well, it wouldn't be long before they showed up. Coming in careless since they expected him to keep on the move.

False dawn was spreading its pale colors over the rugged landscape when Bilo Mackley saw some birds taking wing farther east in the ravine. He got into firing position, made certain there was a shell in the chamber, pushed his hat back a little, and allowed a grim smile to split his lips.

Mist ghosted up from the creek below to obscure Bilo Mackley's view of the canyon. But this was of little concern to him since he could hear Rye Garth cursing the others on. One horse appeared; hunkered in the saddle was Ray Sundby. Sundby kept looking down at the ground, and from this distance of about fifty yards he loomed large in Mackley's gunsight. Still the gunhand waited until another rider appeared, Waddell.

"Just as I figured," he said derisively, "Rye's acting as rearguard again. Damned coward!"

Zeroing in on Sundby's chest, Bilo Mackley squeezed off a shot, and with the reverberating echo of his rifle chasing back what remained of the night, he pulled down on Art Waddell even as Sundby was dropping out of the saddle. Waddell was looking around wild-eyed when that slug punched a hole into his head to rip off his Stetson and cause the bronc he rode to get to bucking and snorting its fear. Though he knew he'd scored a killing shot, Mackley levered his rifle and pumped another steel-jacketed slug into Waddell. Swinging his rifle farther to the east, he waited for Rye Garth to come riding in. Then he heard the retreating thud of hoofs and he spat out disgustedly,

"Figures. No way that cowardly bastard'll come back here. So I might as well hump my butt out of this canyon."

Bilo Mackley walked his horse down to check on the bodies. The horses of the dead gunmen had swung to follow after Rye Garth. He used the barrel of his rifle to turn Ray Sundby over onto his back. Sightless gray eyes peered past Mackley at a crow just beginning to circle overhead. First he checked out the dead man's pockets and took what money he found. He did the same to the other gunhand.

"Sorry about messing up them pretty locks of yours, Art. I'd take your comb but I figure someone like you could have lice."

Climbing into the saddle, he rode slowly out of the ravine, and on some high ground, reined up to sort out his line of travel. Westward, for sure. A

111

good hideout would be around Benson's Landing. Or beyond that at Yellowstone. "Hear them miners ain't no great shucks at gambling. Get on, hoss."

Farther east Rye Garth had holed up at an empty line shack. He kept peering out of an open window expecting Mackley to show at any moment. The sun was up now, but low to the east and blinding to the eye. But all Rye could think about was Bilo Mackley coming after him. He couldn't stop shaking, and felt queasy from all the whiskey he'd drunk last night. Gone was his arrogance, that cocky glint in his eyes.

One moment he was behind them, his gunhands, the next they were spilling out of their saddles. He hadn't expected Mackley to wait for them. Or perhaps he'd expected more from the men he'd hired to do his fighting for him. Above all, there was in Rye Garth this unsettling feeling of being alone out here. Always before his hirelings had been here to keep the barflies away and others who'd like nothing more than to goad him into a fight.

"What now?" he asked anxiously. "And how can I explain to my pa why all that money is missing? Damn you, Mackley, damn you!"

It took Rye Garth another fifteen minutes to gather enough courage to make a break for his horse barely tethered outside the open door of the line shack. He scrambled into saddle, and his spurs gouged into the flanks of his bronc to have it bolt toward a barbed wire fence and almost go through it before its rider could rein away and head it toward the home buildings. As Rye Garth rode, fear often brought him twisting around to scan his backtrail for any sign of the gunhand, Bilo Mackley.

Killing those whores had seen him in command of the situation. It wasn't supposed to be this way, he told himself, and forcing his mind away from the cruel fact of what Mackley had said, that he was no more'n a coward.

Chapter Eleven

Despite the need Sam Chapman had for a hot meal and about a pot of chicory coffee to wash it down, after leaving the 44 he headed back past the courthouse to saddle his horse. From the directions given him by Mag Burns, banker Miller occupied one of those big and mysterious homes sheltered by weeping willows and elms and edging onto the Yellowstone River. He could have walked over to the banker's house, but there was a certain mystique to someone arriving on horseback.

"Let's face it," he murmured upon leaving the livery stable and reining up a narrow lane, "you hate walking of any kind."

Still setting strongly in his mind was the way Judge Garth had acted when he'd called upon Sam in his office. Mag's description of the man who'd committed those murders could just about fit any gunslinger. Whereas the judge had boldly stated he knew who the killer was, as no doubt did Sheriff Toby Pindale. Earlier, while passing along main street on his way to the 44, he'd spotted Pindale and one of his deputies entering one of the saloons. Maybe they had gotten a posse together and gone after the killer of that whore. Lost the trail, then returned to Miles City. First thing in the morning he meant to have a long talk with Toby Pindale, get a few things squared away. It might not do any good since Pindale was Judge Harlan A. Garth's man, body and soul.

"A couple of political soul brothers awright. One scratching the other's back."

First he would come across a red brick house having gimcracks decorating its front porch, Mag had told him. Beyond this would be Charles Miller's big two-story house, and passing down a lane guarded by trees, Sam came upon the house fronted by spreading willow trees. Out in front of the curving driveway a black horse stood harnessed to a surrey, and it seemed every window was throwing out light. White siding covered the walls and he could see someone moving past a gable window just to the right of the front door. Sam hesitated before swinging down, for he'd recognized the surrey as belonging to Doc Waterton. But how could he deny the request of someone who was on his last legs, according to Mag Burns?

Tying the reins to the black metal post, he went up the short flight of steps and swung the door knocker a couple of times. When the door opened, Sam doffed his hat and said,

"I'm Marshal Chapman. Been told that Mr. Miller wants to see me." He could see the anxious look on the face of the maid, a negro woman dressed modestly in a flowing black dress and ruffled white apron. "I've heard that Mr. Miller isn't feeling all that well."

"Please, Marshal, I'll tell them you're here." She stepped aside to allow Sam passage into the high-domed entryway, and closed the door to hurry away.

He felt awkward holding his hat in his hands and staring back at his reflection in a large wall mirror. Until now he hadn't noticed the trail dust barely filming his weathered face and dusting his clothing, but to brush it away would see it falling onto the polished hardwood floor. He could see into the large living room and beyond to a large window gaping out onto the wide expanse of lawn flowing toward the river. There was something to be said for having money, he reckoned. His eyes swung to the maid turning the corner and crooking a beckoning finger.

"My, Mr. Miller is sure anxious to see you, marshal. This way, please."

Now he fixed his eyes on the staircase and banister curling to the second floor landing. And when he touched onto the upper floor, it was to have the maid gesture toward one of the doors farther along the lighted hallway. He went there as Doc Waterton and a woman emerged, with Waterton saying softly, "Marshal, I hope this doesn't take too long."

"Reckon that's up to Mr. Miller."

"Yes. He has been asking about you."

As Sam stepped into the large bedroom, the doctor closed the door behind him. Now he fastened his eyes upon Charley Miller stretched out in the big canopied bed. At a wan hand signal from the banker he moved closer and nodded courteously as he eased onto an overstuffed chair.

"Marshal Chapman . . . I hate being like this . . ." A tired smile flashed out of the banker's eyes. His facial skin had the washed out and ashy appearance of someone barely clinging to life, while his voice had been reedy, hesitant. "Right about now I . . . could use a good snifter of . . . brandy . . . and a fine cigar. I suppose you're wondering why I wanted to see you . . ."

"Mag told me to drop by."

"A good woman, Mag. Better than a lot of them around here."

Sam leaned closer so that he could hear better, and this brought a smile to the banker's face.

"Used to outshout and outtalk most others. So, marshal, I suppose you'd call this . . . confession time."

"You mean you robbed your own bank—"

Charley Miller's eyes sparkled, and he laughed weakly.

Now a somber expression fixed itself on his face. "I haven't much time; a week or two at the most, according to Waterton. If that. He calls what I have, cancer — something that eats away from inside to . . . destroy a man."

"A hard way to go."

"Bear with me now, Marshal Chapman. What I am about to tell you is the unvarnished truth. The truth as I know it, and have learned the hard way, about Judge Garth."

Sam stopped fiddling with his hat as an attentive gleam came into his eyes. He hadn't expected something of this nature. He knew, as did most everyone hereabouts, that Judge Garth was a director at the Citizens Bank. No doubt what Charley Miller had to tell him would involve money, but that would do for starters.

"It all began when George Davine came to see me about extending his loan," stated Banker Charley Miller. "At the time I had every intention of giving Davine all the time he needed to make good on his note. But to my sorrow and misjudgment I listened to Harlan Garth. The man has this uncanny ability to beguile the hell out of a person. So instead of helping rancher George Davine, a vote of our board of directors saw the bank foreclosing on the Clearwater. Afterward, it was Judge Garth who insisted the Clearwater be put into receivership. Then, Marshal Chapman, murder entered into it."

"I'd heard that George Davine had disappeared. Out here that isn't all that uncommon," Chapman said.

"Davine was murdered; no question about that."

"What you're telling me, Mr. Miller, is that Judge Garth could have had a hand in this."

"Exactly!"

"You got any proof to go on?"

"The words of Judge Garth. We were arguing about the way this deal involving the Clearwater Ranch was handled. I . . . I told Garth that he'd used his position as a

118

judge to gain control of the ranch."

"Guess he did at that."

"It was then Judge Garth told me the bare . . . the horrifying facts about how Davine had been murdered. That I was also involved in this . . . in fact was an accessory to the fact . . . because my bank had foreclosed on the Clearwater. I . . . I couldn't think straight. So I . . . kept quiet about this."

"About Garth committing murder?"

"It was Judge Garth—and one of his men who did this—one of those gunhands Garth likes to keep out at the ranch. Yes, Bilo Mackley."

"This is unsettling news, Mr. Miller. But it seems to me all you're guilty of is getting involved with Harlan Garth."

"I'm guilty of being a coward, Marshal Chapman. May God forgive me for this. And . . . and he's a federal judge now. In an untouchable position."

"Any man can be brought down when the truth comes out."

"Perhaps."

"Will you do this for me? Have Doc Waterton place on paper what you just told me," Sam asked.

"Then my wife might find out."

"She might anyway. Consider just who I am, Mr. Miller. Someone who hated hard work and with no future, being appointed to this position. So just telling me about this probably won't carry too much weight."

"Very well, I'll do as you want. What now, marshal?"

"Judge Garth knows the law better'n me. He's an expert at dealing with people . . . and has a lot of power hereabouts. What we need is to find this Bilo Mackley. With Mackley and your statement it'll be curtains for the judge. Can't thank you enough, Charley Miller."

As a rule Sam took his morning meal over at a small

119

cafe, Muriel's Bar & Grill, mostly frequented by drovers, waddies, or plain common folk. Steak and eggs and the trimmings came to two bits. Before getting stuck with this U.S. marshals badge, he'd been able to dine in relative obscurity. Just as he was about to enter the cafe this morning, rubbing the sleep out of his eyes and already savoring that first cup of southern coffee, along had come the editor of the *Yellowstone Journal* to virtually drag Sam over to the Inter Ocean Hotel and its dining room. Another unsettling matter of concern to Sam was the presence of county clerk Otis Plumb at their table. Sam's first tentative sip of the coffee served here told him he'd made a drastic mistake. And the meal, same's as he would have ordered at Muriel's, was doubled in price to four bits. He would have taken his leave had not T.R. McElrath told the waitress to put Sam's breakfast on his tab, and also Otis Plumb's.

"You eat here often?"

"I've acquired a taste for the food served here."

"Food's priced awful high."

"I hadn't noticed."

"Maybe I should have gotten into the newspaper game."

"With all those descriptive phrases you throw around, Sam, I do believe you missed your calling," went on T.R. McElrath.

"Otis, what do you think? T.R. trying to flimflam me again?"

"I'd rather not venture an opinion on that, Sam. But I've eaten here on occasion."

"Okay, you dragged me over here, T.R. Any particular reason?"

"Part of it is about what's been happening lately. These killings. I talked to Mag Burns and her description of the man who knifed her pretty well matches that of a man working out at the Clearwater Ranch."

"Would that be a gunhand named Mackley?"

"It could?"

"Could we talk privately, T.R.?"

"I believe we can include Mr. Plumb in this conversation."

Sam's eyes went to Otis Plumb, sunk in his own thoughts behind the thick lens of his glasses.

"Otis has told me some interesting things about Judge Garth. Enough so that anything we say here will not get back to the courthouse."

Sam's respect for the county clerk went up several notches. Then he settled his mind on Bilo Mackley. The man had been mixed up in an earlier killing while working for the Clearwater Ranch. Afterward, why had Judge Garth kept the gunhand around? Whenever he'd seen Mackley, it had been in the company of Harlan Garth's son, Rye. Perhaps it was because Rye Garth was an irresponsible young man liking to drink and gamble too much. But it didn't make any sense for a man in Judge Garth's eminent position to keep gunhands around. Getting back to last night's startling confession by the banker, Sam knew enough about law to realize that when the chips were down, it would be the banker's word against the judge's. Just telling a man a killing had been done wouldn't sway a jury. What was needed was a corpus delicti. If the former owner of the Clearwater had, as the banker insisted, been murdered, the key to all of this was Bilo Mackley. Right now though, Sam would keep what he'd been told by Charley Miller to himself. Then the editor of the *Yellowstone Journal* cut into his worrying thoughts.

"Otis has told me the judge has been sending letter to someone back east in Chicago."

"Some old flame?"

"Occasionally," broke in Otis Plumb, "the judge will summon me up to do some paperwork; legal work and such. A hard man to please, believe me. But being left alone in the judge's chambers has given me the opportunity to view other matters of a personal nature. Once he had to leave in rather a hurry. In doing so, Judge Garth neglected to lock up this cabinet, something, I might add, he always does. Perhaps I overstepped my, shall you say, the limitations of my trust, when I more or less browsed through the contents of that cabinet. There were various ledgers, old papers, and letters and such. Then I came across this old notebook. In it I found a rather interesting name and address."

"Judge Garth," said McElrath, "has been sending money to a detective with the Chicago Police Department; every month like clockwork."

"Means he's being blackmailed."

"To this end I contacted an old acquaintance now working for a Chicago newspaper. Asked him to run through some old issues of his paper . . . that maybe something interesting happened some half dozen years ago."

"So, Garth was a lawyer there. Big city lawyers aren't noted for their modesty, or honest ways."

"Whatever the reason, Sam, it is apparent that Judge Harlan A. Garth did something wrong. As a newspaperman I owe it to the folks out here to find out just what kind of a federal judge we have."

"In my opinion," muttered Sam, "he's a real mean sonofabitch. But then again, no one ever asks me my opinion. Even those three women I was hitched to never asked for my advice. Sort of saps a man's confidence."

"I'll let you know the minute I come up with something."

"Do that. Now if you don't mind, T.R., I do believe I'll manhandle this expensive breakfast you bought me."

Chapter Twelve

The rest of the day kind of dragged on for Marshal Sam Chapman. While a trip to the court-house revealed that Judge Garth was tied up with legal matters. But one of the clerks did tell Sam that the trial of rustlers Schatz and Bolanger would commence as soon as a jury was impounded. That Sam and his deputies would be called upon to testify against the rustlers.

It had always been a steadfast rule of Sam's that no hard liquor would pass his lips until he'd parta-ken of a noon meal and allowed it to settle. What brought him traipsing into the Diamond Saloon was a brief encounter with one of Sheriff Pindale's depu-ties, this after Sam had gone over to the sheriff's office, to be told that Toby Pindale was closeted with Judge Garth.

At the bar, just newly made in St. Louis and shipped out here on a riverboat, Sam found some space between three cowhands to his left and oppo-site a spatted and suited salesman trying to sell some cheap jewelry to one of the barmaids. Neither parties cast the new arrival any curious glances. The music didn't help Sam's disposition either, the rail-thin chap seated at the piano beating out a loud version of "Buffalo Gal." While waiting for one of the bardogs to drift over, he peered over his shoulder at six men hunkered around a poker table. He envied every man jack of them, even the waddy who'd just thrown his hand down in disgust. That was the life. Tobacco smoke burning your eyes, the clicking of poker chips, bluffing 'cause the cards you held were maybe a pair of deuces against some undecided gent holding a trio of tens.

"Sam, where the hell you been?"

"Right here for about six months waiting for you to drift over, Elmo."

"How's the marshaling business?"

"Tolerably painful."

"Expect that, what with you being saddled with rustlers for deputies. If it weren't for this wooden leg, Sam, I'd be siding you out there."

"That sure eases my mind a lot, Elmo."

"The usual?" The barkeep reached for a beer stein.

"That, and some whiskey to cleanse my mind."

"Expect there'll be a trial soon."

"Not soon enough for me, Elmo."

The first sip of cold beer didn't taste all that bad, though for some reason the whiskey caused him to frown, and then to set the whiskey bottle aside. His, Sam was beginning to realize, was a very perilous occupation. In the days since he'd been made a lawman, he'd been bringing to mind and casting away any number of reasons why he should be wearing this badge. Now he knew there was only one explanation, and one so obvious that he'd overlooked it. Judge Garth needed someone he could handle, a man raw to the law business, and with a questionable background like Sam's. Someone who could be manipulated. And worse yet, someone to pin the blame on if and when the truth about Judge Harlan Garth came out.

"Seems that's you, old hoss."

Adding salt to his wounds was the judge not being able to see him. And all the time Sheriff Pindale had been up in the judge's chambers. It could only be they were having over what to do about Bilo Mackley. Gnawing at Sam as he motioned for Elmo to refill his empty beer glass was just how to approach Judge Garth. He wasn't about to go over there and drag Garth to the Basement Felony. Though it was a thoughtful morsel that he chewed on for a few minutes. Here he was, coming onto middle-age where a man should know better, and being saddled with a badge and petty crooks for deputies. Here he had to answer to a man having bloodstained hands. For a fact Harlan Garth had more brazen gall than any man Sam had met before. Plus the grudging fact Garth always seemed to have a leg up on others out here as far as legal jurisprudence was concerned. It just could be that if he made a move to arrest the judge, the tables could be turned through some legal maneuvering and it would be Marshal Sam Chapman occupying a cell in Basement Felony.

"Just thinkin' all this marlarky through gets my head to aching," he complained, and with that Sam shoved his drink aside and tramped over sawdust to the batwings.

Sam held to the shadows fringing along the boardwalk, with the aromatic scent of tobacco fetching him into Pederson's Tobacco Shop; there he laid a critical eye upon the proprietor adjusting his dark red suspenders. "You're sure packin' on the weight,

Walt. Yup, another pound or two and you'll have a tough time wedging yourself behind that counter. These fresh cigars?"

"Just came in . . . and generally they're free to starpackers. But after your kind words, Sam, a nickel-a-cigar."

"Don't mind paying my own freight around here. What's the latest news?" Sam swiped a wooden match along the counter and when it flamed, lit his cigar.

"Just that the railroad is fixing to lay track out of Bismarck most anytime. And you know about that whore getting killed, I expect."

"Bad thing."

"It doesn't help my business any."

"You mean these women of the night come in here to buy cigars? That is news."

This brought a chuckle from Pederson, and he said, "It's a wonder you've lived this long, Sam. But seriously, word is the killer is a gunhand named Mackley. And is it also gospel fact Mackley worked out at the Clearwater?"

"More or less, that is, if you can call sitting around and drinking or wetnursing Rye Garth work."

"Should know better than to ask you about work, Sam, since it's been your lifelong passion to avoid it."

Laughing, Sam said, "Guess I'm not the only one who's packing on some weight; but mine's more in the area of my mouth. Seen my deputies around?"

"Earlier this morning. How do you handle them?"

"On a short leash, Walt. Well, best be ambling on. And give my regards to the missus—tell Carol, too, that she puts too much seasoning in her gou-

126

lash."

When Sam walked out into noonday sunlight, it was to be hailed by one of the court employees, and somewhat reluctantly he broke stride. When the man stated that Judge Garth wanted to see him, though Sam nodded courteously; in him was this sudden flare of resentment. Last night Judge Garth seemed more concerned with his personal matters than the fact Sam and his deputies had brought back those rustlers. What further rankled him was Garth not telling him Mag Burns had been hurt.

"I'll be over soon's I chow down."

"The judge won't like that, Marshal Chapman. He said to bring you over right away."

"Unclog them ears, son. After I get some vittles." He turned and walked away. Only when Sam Chapman had downed a meal of beef stew and sour-dough biscuits at an upstreet cafe did he begin that long southerly walk down main street to the court-house. Along the way he glanced in a few saloons and gambling dens for any sign of his deputies, then he was inside the courthouse and sauntering toward Judge Harlan A. Garth's chambers on the second floor.

He was accosted by a vinegar-faced woman in the outer office. Under her disapproving eyes he managed to remove his Stetson, then it was a case of who would speak first, until the silence was broken by the judge yelling out of his inner office, "Is that Chapman?"

Unzippering her thin lips, she said icily, "The judge wants to see you."

"Did you learn that by close observation," he said pleasantly, along with throwing the woman a couple of winks. He stepped past her desk over the old carpeting and across the threshold. The room didn't seem as large as before, or it could be this was due more to what Sam now felt about the man who'd appointed him a U.S. marshal. At an impatient gesture from the judge, Sam draped his large frame over a chair planted before the large desk. He remained silent, letting his eyes flick from Judge Garth scrawling words on a yellowed sheet of paper to an elm tree rustling just outside the open window.

"As I've told you before, Chapman, this territory is infested with rustlers. I'm pleased that you caught two of them. But rather than having you wait around to testify at their trial, it is my decision to have you head out as soon as possible. An affidavit from you and your deputies will suffice as to how you captured Schatz and Bolanger. Your other deputies took those horses back to the Bar D; expect they'll show up later today or tomorrow."

"I expect so. What about these killings? That girl of Mag's and . . ."

"Since that happened locally, Chapman, finding the killer will rest in the hands of Sheriff Pindale."

"I've a personal stake in this, Judge Garth. Mag's pretty sure the killer is a gunhand named Bilo Mackley."

"As I told you, marshal, leave finding Mackley to our sheriff."

"That killing may have been done here, your honor, but by now Mackley has taken off for the wide open bonies, meaning my jurisdiction."

Judge Garth threw his quilled pen down and planted his fists on his desk top as his eyes chiseled, and he said coldly and carefully, "Mackley is not a rustler. I appointed you specifically to hunt down

128

rustlers. Lord man, local ranchers are breathing down my neck about their horses and cattle being stolen. What I'm saying is that these men don't care if some whore gets killed. Do I make myself clear?"

"Clear as a mud fence," Sam said bitterly.

"If you don't feel up to the job?"

There it was, an invitation to shuck this badge and job and go back to what he knew best. But Sam Chapman knew he couldn't let go now. Not with what he knew about the judge. As for Judge Garth ordering him not to go after Bilo Mackley, it could only mean that Garth didn't want the man brought back alive. If that happened, the statement made by banker Charley Miller would have little meaning. Framing a smile, he said, "You're ramrodding the law hereabouts. So it's after rustlers we'll be a-going."

"Before you leave, marshal, give your statement on rustlers Schatz and Bolanger to Miss Chilburn."

The bold orders from the judge that Marshal Chapman and his men head out right away to hunt down more rustlers meant one thing to Sam: that neither Garth nor Sheriff Toby Pindale knew where gunhand Mackley was hiding out. It could be here in Miles City, south someplace on the Clearwater Ranch or, and this was Sam's opinion, Mackley'd gone westward.

Town air felt good once Sam had left the courthouse. His first order of business was checking out the whereabouts of deputies Glover and McVay, and he knew they wouldn't be too happy about having to head out pronto. He figured the others would come riding in by sundown.

129

One of the legal matters the judge had gone over with Sam were the readers he carried on known rustlers. The judge had told him that his first move should be to head out to the country around the Judith Basin as it was a hotbed of rustling activity. He knew the country well, having done a little gambling at such cowtowns as Roundup, Harlowton, Musselshell. There were the Judith Mountains, the Little Rockies, of course Big Snow Mountain lying just to the east of the Little Belts. Plenty of secluded places for rustlers to hold cattle or horses until they found a buyer.

But this country was hardly the place a gunhand like Bilo Mackley would head to lie low for a spell. He wanted Mackley, bad. Because in Sam Chapman was this silent rage over what had happened to Mag Burns. She meant a lot to him. But as for getting hitched, Sam had pretty much closed the door on such notions. Though she treated him better'n others around Miles City.

As for Bilo Mackley, he would probably make tracks for a place where he could pick up some easy money. Westward a tumbling of mining camps lay in the valleys or up amongst the high plateaus. Raw settlements having virtually no law were gathering places for high rollers, con artists, and men on the dodge. This was where Mackley would go. And taking out after him, Sam knew with a grim certainty, would be Sheriff Toby Pindale. He knew Pindale as a lackadaisical sort, average with a gun, which meant that when Sheriff Pindale did take out after Mackley it would be with some hired guns of his own. Pindale would have to leave some of his deputies behind to keep law and order. It would be the more resourceful Judge Garth who would take care of hiring these gunslingers, for if Pindale had any choice in the matter he would stay here in Miles City and forget about finding Bilo Mackley. The man wanted to be sheriff; now it was time for Pindale to pay back his political dues to the judge.

"But if I get to Mackley first," pondered Sam, "The real loser in this killing game is gonna be Harlan Garth."

There had always been in Kiley Glover this reckless streak. Let him have a few drinks and that wild talking of his usually found Glover being hammered into sawdust or asked to step out behind some saloon. Ever since returning to Miles City, Glover and Joe McVay had been making the rounds of the saloons and other places serving drinks or catering to gamblers. It was around ten o'clock last night that found Kiley Glover getting into a poker game over at The Busted Elbow, a shady gambling den run by a one-eyed French-Canadian. Though the game had seen some busted and leaving and others coming in to try their luck, Glover had managed to stay even until around mid-morning, when his luck seemed to change abruptly. He'd taken five pots running, a fact noted by the other players, and Joe McVay seated alone at a nearby table.

McVay could handle his whiskey. Even so, he liked to nurse his drinks, and words. Him and Kiley Glover had grown up together, hardscrabble places just north of the Yellowstone Basin. Long ago McVay had lost any illusions he'd had about women and life in general. It was almost happenstance them drifting into a wayward way of getting by, since neither of them particularly liked hiring on as cowhands nor working for freight drovers. Unlike the more casual attitude of Kiley Glover, deputy marshal McVay never took anything for granted. He treated his horse and weapons with equal respect, tending to them first before seeing to his personal needs. Whenever he had a few spare minutes McVay would head out by himself and practice his draw and accuracy with sixgun and rifle. This was something he kept to himself, as Joe McVay did his innermost feelings. Another part of his quiet and brooding nature was always to observe carefully everything that was happening around him. Sometimes one of the barmaids would stop at his table for a few words, and now he said to one of them, "That hombre hogging the front end of the bar, ever seen him before?"

"He's a stranger to me, Joe."

Nodding, McVay spun his empty shot glass around where he sat slouched in the hardbacked wooden chair, one boot hooked up on another. Somewhat tall, weathered-out face, hard eyes, was his silent assessment of the newcomer up by the bar, with all the earmarks of a gunhand. The newcomer had aroused McVay's curiosity simply because of his marked interest in the poker game involving Kiley Glover. While in that game was another drifter with the same ear-notchings. Partners in crime, he'd figured out. Miles City was no stranger to men like this, still, in Joe McVay was this uneasiness, though you couldn't tell anything was troubling him by glancing at McVay's unruffled face and the easy way he picked up the whiskey bottle and poured another drink.

Another smirking laugh tore out of Kiley Glover as he reached out with both arms and began raking in another bunch of poker chips. In the last hour alone he'd bought drinks around a couple of times, and now he caught the eye of a passing barmaid and uttered happily, "Give these gents what they crave, Mabel."

"Another new deck of cards," complained a pudgy cowpoke. "Glover, if you ain't the luckiest sonofagun I've seen in a long time, I swear."

"Generally it's me doin' the bitching, Curly. Hotdamn though, them cards is sure running."

"Maybe this change of luck is due to that new job you've got. How does it feel to be doing honest work for a change?"

"Being a deputy marshal is sure different, I tell you."

"Where's your badge?"

"Tucked away in my vest pocket. Well, whose deal is it?"

"Mine," groused another player. He took a new deck of cards from the barmaid and broke the seal on the pack as he added, "Glover, maybe this'll break that lucky run of yours."

"Maybe it isn't luck," intoned a hawkfaced man seated across the table from Glover.

"What's that supposed to mean?"

"Could be, Glover, you've been cheating," went on the hawkfaced gent as he placed both hands on the green felt cloth.

"Cheating?" Kiley Glover laughed. "I ain't even any good at riffling them cards, let alone one to cheat."

"I say you are!"

"That's it for me," mumbled Curly the cowhand as he scooped up the few chips he had left and shoved his chair away from the table. The other

133

players eased out of their chairs to leave only two men seated at the poker table, Glover and the hawkfaced man.

"Mister," spat out Glover, "I beat you square and fair. An' I won't be called a card cheater by no man."

A few moments ago Marshal Sam Chapman had completed his search of main street and a few side streets for his deputies. Now, swinging onto a narrow lane up on the northern edges of the business district, he bypassed some horses idling out in front of the Busted Elbow Saloon and sought the batwings. He was still brushing past the batwings when it struck Sam that it was awful quiet in this saloon. He held there, instantly alert, taking in the two men confronting one another at a back card table.

"Be damned if Glover hasn't gotten himself into trouble," Sam said, and then saw another stranger standing near the front end of the long bar where it crooked around, the man had unleathered his Smith & Wesson and was holding it low at his side. "Two against one don't seem fair."

Casually Sam swung toward the bar and eyed the man holding the gun before he muttered quietly, "Nice day for a killing."

The man blinked in surprise.

"I'm not wearing this badge just to ward off evil spirits," Sam went on. "Just ease that Smith & Wesson you're holding up here on the bar or suffer the consequences."

"And if I don't?"

Sam jerked a thumb over at Joe McVay taking in what was happening at the bar and by the poker table. "His name's McVay. One of my deputies. All

134

McVay knows is killing. Meaning that while you're thinking about where to shoot me or if the light is about right in here or anything else, all McVay has on his mind is blowing your lights out. Any other questions?"

The gunhand brought up his arm and laid the gun gently upon the bartop, and with Sam picking up the weapon and tucking it into his belt. "Go sit over there where I can keep an eye on you, hombre." He stepped away from the bar, and it was then Sam recalled just who it was Kiley Glover was facing at the poker table. Despite himself, and the fact it was tolerably warm in this saloon, a cold sliver of uneasiness rippled at him. "Last time I saw you, Tonto Blair, was down at Cheyenne."

The gunhand stepped so that he could watch both Glover and Sam at the same time. "Yeah, ain't you Chapman?" His careful and gray-filmed eyes took in McVay hovering off to his right, the other gunhand just settling somewhat unhappily onto a chair, and flicked back to Sam. "That badge must get awful heavy at times."

"Packing it can be a chore. What's the problem?"

"This sodbuster was cheating."

"Ain't so, Sam. I won these chips on the up and up."

"Kiley, I believe you." Sam knew it wasn't mere happenstance these gunhands showing up here at Miles City. They could be, and if his hunch was right, those hired by Judge Garth. Which meant they had come here deliberately to pick a fight with his deputies. Proving this was another matter.

"It's your move, Chapman."

"Well, Mr. Tonto Blair, today I'm in a tolerable mood. Both of us know my deputy wasn't cheating

135

at cards and . . ."

"Meaning you're calling me a liar?"

"Meaning you made a mistake. Meaning that if you keep on jawing away, Tonto Blair, I'm gonna have to arrest you for defying this here U.S. marshal's badge. It's your move."

The gunhand said, "That's right Chapman, hide behind that badge."

Without warning, a gun sounded, and when everyone spun that way, they saw Joe McVay standing there with his smoking gun. Cursing and clutching at his hand was the other gunhand, the hideout gun he'd drawn lying at his feet.

Then through the batwings came a couple of deputy sheriffs followed by Sheriff Toby Pindale. It took a moment for Pindale to find out how things lay here at the Busted Elbow, but in that brief time Sam Chapman realized that Sheriff Pindale had sent these gunmen out to harass his deputies. Sam fought to control his temper as he stared back at the sheriff.

"That's what happens, Chapman, when you turn rustlers into lawmen; they just can't keep out of trouble."

"You let me worry about that, sheriff," Sam said cuttingly.

"Speaking of worrying," came back Pindale, "that's what you should be doing. Seems some Bar D hands just brought in one of your deputies, Tugwell, I believe. Took Tugwell's body over to the funeral home. Well, McVay, I suggest you holster that gun and make tracks out of here. Or I could just arrest you now and let you spend a few days in jail."

"Easy, Pindale," Sam muttered as he motioned for

his deputies to leave. "Trouble with you damned Republicans is that you want to become kings and dukes and worse."

Outside, he fell into step with Glover and McVay, the worry of their thoughts showing on their faces, and then McVay said, "All I can figure is that Mort Reiser had a hand in this."

"You mean . . . he killed Chili?"

"Yup, Kiley, as Mort was always the sneaky type."

"Let's try to find those Bar D hands," suggested Sam.

Which they did, at a saloon farther south on main street. The two waddies and three lawmen commandeered a back table at Taylor's Olde Tyme Tavern, a favorite hangout of most cowmen, and quickly they learned the details of how Chili Tugwell's body had been found up north close to Great Porcupine Creek.

"He was shot at close range," said one of the hands. "Then left for the buzzards. Whoever did it took those horses Tugwell was bringing back."

"That would be Mort Reiser," Glover said grimly. "Should have braced him long before this. My not doing so cost Chili his life."

"Boys, I appreciate you bringing in the body. And I'm sorry those horses got stolen again."

"Not your fault, marshal."

"Chili, he wasn't a bad sort." Sam shrugged tiredly and looked around the table. "As for Reiser, we know where he'll probably head with those hosses. Which means, gents, I'll be heading out come sunup."

"Not without me."

"Same here."

"You're still my deputies, awright. Done good so

far. But where I'll be heading is a heap more dangerous place than out on the prairie."

"And me and Joe'll be right alongside you, Sam. That's all fact."

Chapter Thirteen

Judge Harlan Garth brought his covered surrey away from one of the lanes that served as a thoroughfare for ranchers coming into Miles City from the southwest. Passing by an old mossy-barked oak, he reined down a rutted track running through a cut in the river bank. There was still enough sunlight to allow the judge to swing his surrey around. Drawing up, he scanned the clayey stretch of level ground fringing onto the water for fresh hoofmarkings. This passage down to the river was one of several townfolks used when they came fishing or just to get a closer view of the Yellowstone. But it was the only one guarded by an oak tree.

While waiting somewhat impatiently for Tonto Blair to put in an appearance, Garth mused over the disturbing news of Marshal Chapman being seen entering the home of banker Charles Miller. He knew the banker was seriously ill. He'd learned that Miller could only be pushed so far. Perhaps it had been a mistake on his part in telling the banker that he'd had a hand in the death of George Davine. So it could be Miller had told the marshal about this just to purge his soul. Once Chapman had left Miles City in search of rustlers, it would be a good thing to call upon Charley Miller and set things right.

When a horseman put in an appearance east along the river, Garth tied up the reins and got out of the surrey. Then gunhand Tonto Blair cantered up and dismounted. "What's so important, judge?"

"I want to know why you went after Chapman's deputies?"

"That was the sheriff's idea," Blair said indifferently.

"I thought so. You know what to do when you find Bilo Mackley—"

"You must want Mackley dead awful bad."

"Just do it. I'm paying you enough."

Tonto Blair stooped to pick up a flat stone, then he underhanded it out onto the river. The stone skipped across the murky surface before slowing down and sinking. In the eyes of the gunhand was a speculating gleam. This was how he had this figured: the sheriff was just one of the judge's sycophantic yes men, but what the judge probably hadn't told Sheriff Pindale was they'd be carting a dead body back to Miles City. All he knew about Mackley was local talk of how the man had killed some whore. That, in Tonto Blair's estimation, didn't call for Mackley to be shot outright. Blair had also learned that Mackley had been working out at the judge's Clearwater Ranch. Which brought to mind a question that had been plaguing Blair ever since he'd been summoned here, and that was why a federal judge would keep a hired gun on the payroll. Perhaps he should just be satisfied with the money he'd be making out of this instead of trying to figure all of this out.

"One other thing. Pindale may know his way around the back alleys and cathouses of Miles City, but it's a different kind of action westward."

"The sheriff will be in charge, Blair. I know, Pindale has his limitations, but I doubt if Mackley will hand his guns over to a man with your reputation."

"Reckon not, judge. You're awful certain Mackley will strike for those mining camps?"

"Reasonably certain."

"Well, I ain't learned nothing new out here. Just why did you want this powwow?"

"As you said, Mr. Blair, our sheriff has his limitations. Once you find Mackley, the sheriff could interfere — try to bring him back alive. Then you just might have to bring back more'n one body."

The following morning, word was brought to Judge Garth that the president and major stock-holder of the Citizens Bank of Miles City had passed away. Earlier, and from an office window, he'd watched Sheriff Toby Pindale pass quietly along main street on his way to find gunhand Bilo Mackley. There had been no sign of Marshal Chapman, and Garth surmised the marshal could have headed out yesterday.

Then, as Judge Garth brushed through the front doors on his way to dinner, the sight of his son, Rye, and segundo Phil Brady and a pair of cowhands riding up, brought him down the walkway and by a hitchrail. He stared up at Rye Garth and said,

"Well, you just couldn't stay out at the ranch."

"There's been trouble," said Phil Brady.

Swinging down, Rye Garth said, "I suppose you're wondering why Waddell and Sundby aren't tagging along?"

"Yes, where are your shadows?"

"Gunned down by Bilo Mackley!"

"That's right," affirmed Brady, "Mackley came out to the ranch. First he forced Rye to open the safe. Took what money there was and headed out."

"We went after him, me and Waddell and Sundby. But we didn't figure Mackley to bushwhack us."

"Can't figure Mackley turning on the Clearwater."

"You can once I tell you that Bilo Mackley killed one of Mag Burns's whores—used a knife on her. You boys get yourselves some chow. I want a word with my son."

Watching the others ride away, Rye Garth said, "Mackley sure enough went against the grain, Pa, by killing that whore. I guess the reason he came out to the ranch was to get some money, and then try to find a hole to crawl into."

"Son, guess I owe you an apology. Those other whores getting killed, and all along it was Mackley. But we'll find him."

"It still hurts, Pa, you feeling I had a hand in those killings."

"We all make mistakes. But it'll be different now, I swear. As for my meddling in running the Clearwater, that'll come to a stop too. You're what, twenty-seven?"

"Closing on it."

"Your mother, may she rest in peace, always kept track of such things. I was just thinking, Rye, about you and Brady going over to Billings to buy some more Oregon cattle. Well, there I go meddling again."

Still burning in Rye Garth was a deep resentment mingled with a release of the worry which he'd kept stored up. It was over now. Sooner or later they'd catch up with Bilo Mackley. Meanwhile it would be up to him to try and control these dark passions that were threatening to destroy him. He was still troubled by the violent deaths of those gunhands, and his own hesitant actions. Yes, perhaps the judge was right, a trip to Billings would get him away, at least temporarily, from the Clearwater and some bitter memories.

"You figure on staying over?"

"Thought we would."

"Good," smiled Judge Garth, "good. I'm buying dinner, son. Then perhaps tonight we can get together."

The sight of Judge Harlan A. Garth getting out of his surrey brought Clarice Miller away from the window and to open the front door. She was dressed in black, with her face showing her grief over the passing of her husband. She couldn't help noticing that the judge had donned a somber black suit, and hesitantly she said, "How nice of you to come, Judge Garth."

"I would have been here sooner, Clarice, but this new job of mine is very trying." He knew her to be a shy woman, not liking to mingle socially at a lot of functions put on by the neighborhood wives, and a woman not prone to gossip. He felt Clarice Miller

143

had led a sheltered life, that it pivoted around her husband. From the way she had greeted him, Harlan Garth sensed that she knew little if nothing about her husband's business dealings.

"Please, come in, Judge Garth."

He entered behind her and closed the door, and holding his hat followed Clarice Miller into the spacious living room. "This is such an exquisite house."

"Charley loved it so. The . . . the visitation will be tomorrow."

"I shall be there. I trust you're holding up at such a bad time." He eased down onto an overstuffed chair. "I know this is also a bad time to ask about banking business, Clarice. But I was told the marshal dropped in the other evening."

"Yes, he did. For a few minutes. At Charley's request."

"Did he mention what they talked about?"

"Oh, heavens no, Charley never discussed business with me. But later, after Marshal Chapman left, Charley asked me to bring him some writing paper. I did so. Then I left him alone with Doc Waterton."

"Afterward, did your husband give you any papers to hold?"

"No, not afterward. But when I went in it seemed to me Doc Waterton was placing some papers in his coat pocket. But you know doctors, they're always handing out prescriptions for this and that."

"Reason I'm asking you this, Clarice," he lied, "is that your husband and I were involved in some banking matters. But, in any case, this is a time of mourning . . . not a time to burden you down anymore."

It was drawing onto ten that evening before a wagon escorted by three cowboys came in off the flats and wended through the streets of Miles City seeking the home of Doc Ben Waterton. In the wagon bed tended by another waddy lay the still form of cowboy Ab Maguire. Every so often a low moan would come from Maguire; other than that he lay huddled under the woolen blankets. Just before coming in off the herd ground out at the K-C Ranch he'd had the misfortune to encounter an Oregon bull trying to get at one of the cows. Somehow the bull had turned on Maguire trying to rein his bronc out of the way. Next thing he knew his horse was down and the bull was butting in to drive one of its horns into Maguire's midriff. Afterward all anyone else could do was bundle Ab Maguire into one of the wagons and make tracks for Miles City.

"This is it."

"You sure?"

"Don't you recall, got my busted leg set here last year by Waterton." The waddy reined up by the picket fence, and swinging down, he hurried up the stone walkway to rap on the white panes of the front door. Moments later a woman called out, then a light showed in one of the bedrooms.

The first thing Rose Waterton noticed when she was roused by the loud knocking was the absence of her husband in their bed. Then she lit one of the lamps before calling out through the open window. "Who is it?"

"Ma'am, one of our boys got hisself trampled and gored by a bull."

"Be right there." Picking up the lamp, Rose Waterton padded on bare feet out into the living room. Then something made her turn toward a corridor down which Doc Waterton's office and waiting room were located. For a moment the shock of what she was seeing, her husband just stumbling out of his office and groping toward her, choked off the scream. Blood stained the doctor's nightgown, but it was the scalpel protruding from his chest that held her eyes.

"Rose . . . help me . . ." He crumbled to the floor.

"No!" she screamed as the lamp dropped out of her hands.

"Something wrong?" The waddy rapped again, then he wrenched the door open and hurried inside.

A block south of Doc Waterton's house a frightened Harlan A. Garth clutched at his bleeding arm as he trotted out of an alley and pulled up to get his bearings. He'd had no other choice but to go over to Waterton's and get that incriminating piece of evidence, Charley Miller's statement against him. And he'd found it tucked inside a ledger resting in a desk drawer. Then Waterton had to stumble in, to cry out, "You?"

This had left Garth with no other choice than to grab for a scalpel, and they'd grappled, with him getting cut on the arm before he managed to drive the weapon into Doc Waterton's chest. Panicking, he'd managed to wrench open a window and get through it, knowing even as he was fleeing that he'd given the doctor a mortal wound.

146

Now he cursed himself and muttered, "I should have made sure . . . I should have made sure he was dead. But . . . no time for this now."

Judge Garth hurried down the street driven by the fear pounding through his veins and found his tethered horse. In the saddle he pointed it toward his large and gloomy house standing by itself on the western outskirts of Miles City.

Upon arriving there and leaving his saddled horse in the small barn, he hurried into his house and burned the damaging piece of paper before tending to his arm wound.

Throughout the long night he spent the time mostly pacing his bedroom floor, and even before daylight came upon the flood basin he was dressed and on his way to the courthouse. Though the wound hadn't been all that deep, he knew stitches would be required, but that could come later. Then, as it was coming onto nine in the morning, courthouse employees began trickling in, and with Otis Plumb telling everyone that Doc Waterton had been murdered.

"Murdered? By whom?"

"Right now they figure some petty crook did it. Place almost caught fire too, but some cowhands tended to that."

At that moment Judge Harlan Garth knew he was home free, which somehow lessened the pain coming from his wound. There were two other doctors here in Miles City. But over in Big Timber he knew of one who owed him a favor, and around midmorning Judge Garth caught the westbound stage.

Now it all came down to them finding Bilo

Mackley, were the judge's smug thoughts as the stagecoach rolled through a portion of the flood plain before spilling up a road and onto prairieland.

"Care for a cigar?"

Judge Garth glanced over at the carpetbagger, and then he smiled at the man and said expansively, "Yes, though I don't indulge all that often, and I thank you, sir. Yes, isn't it a beautiful day."

Chapter Fourteen

It took almost a week of steady riding for Marshal Chapman to proclaim they were coming to the Great Bend of the Yellowstone. Along the way there'd been brief stops at Big Timber, once to view Pompey's Pillar, on to ride through other towns hugging along the river. They no longer wore their badges, just this grim determination on the part of Sam to find Bilo Mackley, and Kiley Glover and Joe McVay to renew old friendships with Mort Reiser.

And also along the way Sam Chapman had tried to give his deputies a cram course in gunhandling and just what to expect in places where there was no law to speak of. Sam had aged into his late thirties thinking he was more'n adequate with the weaponry he toted around. His opinion of Glover was that the man better stick to his Winchester rifle. All he had for Joe McVay was open admiration, and his admonition, "Where the hell did you learn to handle a sixgun like that?"

He'd said this after McVay had riddled an empty bean can Sam had tossed into the air, kept it skydancing and tumbling along the ground before his hammer clicked upon an empty chamber.

"An' your draw spooks me too."

"Spent considerable time practicing."

"Guess you have."

"Must have been, Joe, when I weren't around," said Glover as an admiring smile curved across his mouth.

"Reckon the way you handle that .45 Peacemaker cancels out that reader I sent out on you," Sam said grudgingly. "No question about that. Only thing I've got to ask, Joe, if you ever threw down on a man?"

"Still haven't done that," he admitted.

"Think you can?"

"Haven't done all this practicing just to be called fast. The time comes, Marshal Chapman, I'll draw blood. Just hope it's Reiser's."

There was no hesitation in Sam's voice when he said, "I figure you'll do that awright . . . and to some others needin' a little bloodletting."

That had been two days ago, about where the Clark Fork River joined with the Yellowstone. They were overshadowed by mountain ranges, southward the Bridgers and opposite across the Yellowstone the Crazies. The flood basin had narrowed between sheer foothills. It had warmed into the seventies, one of those hazy summer days where a man would rather go fishing or lie about than be saddlebound. They had cold-camped at noon, and along the way kept their horses to an easy canter to keep them fresh. Out here a man riding a tired horse was oftentimes a dead man. This had been true just a few years earlier, Sam knew, when this was pure quill Indian country. And it held true now, what with all these rustlers and where they were heading, a plentiful sprinkling of highwaymen going after the miners or unwary travelers.

"What you thinking, boys?"

"How life has so many twists and turns."

"True, Kiley."

"Like me toting a badge . . . an' being on speakin' terms with a lawman."

"What about you, Joe?"

"That I've got to stop soon and take a leak."

Though Sam laughed along with Glover, inwardly he realized deputy McVay didn't let the mundane things of life get under his skin. All along he felt there was something different about Joe McVay. Maybe a dark side to the young man. But with a grim certainty Sam knew that when guns began barking, and this could be when they reached Benson's Landing, anyone who had the misfortune to accost McVay could soon be breathing his last.

"Benson's Landing," commented, Sam, "now there's a dark old hole."

"Fill us in on the place."

As Sam Chapman had just mentioned, the little settlement of Benson's Landing was a hard hole. It came into existence because an enterprising gent named Billy Lee built a crude ferry to accommodate people traveling between Bozeman or Fort Ellis and the Crow Agency at the mouth of Mission Creek some fifteen miles farther down the river. Later on Buckskin Williams built a strong drink parlor and trading post, and then Amos Benson and Dan Naleigh opened another, as did another venturesome soul named Countryman. These log huts were on the north side of the river as the south bank was on the Crow Reservation. Benson's landing was the rendezvous of all the thieves and bummers in the country who gambled, peddled whiskey, or bought goods issued to the Indians and stolen horses. As squaw men and those running the saloons kept trading with one another, the situation at the Great Bend of the Yellowstone couldn't be controlled by the U.S. Army.

"So, boys," went on Sam, "don't figure on gettin' any cordial welcome."

It wasn't until late afternoon that the lawmen found themselves viewing chimney smoke and some distant buildings. Sam studied what was going on through his field glass. Once in a while someone would appear, and there were a few horses in the pair of pole corrals, along with a brown horse tied up before the trading post. Shortly thereafter Sam scoped a Crow Indian coming out and climbing aboard the horse and loping southward along the riverbank.

"Seems peaceful enough," said McVay.

"Nightfall is when this place goes wild. River's kind of deep here; but we'll have to cross over." Sam replaced the field glass in a saddlebag and buckled the straps as he went behind his deputies, letting their horses ease down the crumbling bank to the water's edge.

They clung to their saddles as their horses fought the sluggish current in an angled swim that carried them farther away from Benson's Landing. But they made it without mishap. Before crossing they'd removed their boots and held them overhead with their holstered sidearms and now they put on these necessary adornments.

"I could use a drink," muttered Kiley Glover.

"All of us could," Sam agreed. "But sparingly."

"From what you told us, Sam, you were here before—"

"Just as an overnighter. Glad to leave the ticks and Benson's Landing behind. Doubt if anybody would remember me. Just thinking about the place, though, gets me to itching."

"From what I've heard, Marshal Chapman, marriage did that to you too."

"A man's rep sure gets around. Remember, you wastrels, all we want is some word as to where we can find those we're after. Probably be costly; but payin' out a few dinero is better'n gunplay."

Joe McVay, as he pulled alongside Glover, glanced the opposite way at Chapman, and McVay said thoughtfully, "If Mort Reiser did bring them hosses out here just to sell them to the Ojeda gang, he could have spilled the beans about us coming after him, I mean . . ."

"Gave them our general description?" pondered Sam. "Guess we'll just have to cross that bridge when we come to it, Joe. How's this for openers? Kiley hanging out of sight with that rifle of his?"

"I'm powerful thirsty," said Glover, "but it might be to our advantage them figurin' there's only two of us."

"Give us a half hour or so. Then if all hell don't break loose, come a-riding on in."

They parted from Kiley Glover, veering toward higher ground and dense fir trees. Once Sam and McVay had cleared the trees fringing close to the river, they studied the settlement being dusted by sunlight piercing through fluffy white clouds. Besides the corrals and saloons, there were a few log cabins and outhouses spilled about haphazardly, unpainted buildings weathered so they looked old and crumbly. This was a place having little pride, but filled with danger for outsiders and any lawman foolhardy enough to come riding in. Sam pondered over this as they brought their horses onto a worn track following the river. From force of habit he brought his right hand down to caress the butt of his sidearm.

"Which place should we try?"

"Let's try that trading post," answered Sam. In coming to one of the corrals he reined over and checked out the brands on the horses. A couple were Indian ponies and a few broncs were un-branded, the rest carrying brands unfamiliar to both of them. To the west a rider emerged from a dense stand of pine trees leading a packhorse, and closer it turned out to be a trapper, a man clad in buckskin. Both of them swung down in front of the large log structure and tied up their horses.

Just above the main entrance someone had nailed a large elk horn rack. A summery breeze passed through the open door as did Sam and McVay, but a little more cautiously. There didn't seem to be anyone around until McVay nudged Sam while nodding toward a round table beyond which some-one sat wedged in a corner. For a moment they thought the sleeping man was just a corpse, then he passed wind and both of them grimaced.

"A classy joint."

"Seems someone's heard us."

Stepping through a back doorway and hitching at his suspenders came a man Sam remembered as Buckskin Williams. The owner of the trading post wore a heavy woolen shirt rolled up to his elbows,

154

above that a beard seemed to cover most of his face except for the forehead and crafty eyes above the long nose. He stopped behind the cluttered counter and hawked to clear his throat.

"The bar's open," he said, and gesturing to a wide inner doorway. Now his attention was caught by that trapper's shadow falling across the front doorsill. "Howdy, Clem Wayland. Didn't expect you this soon."

"Needed flour and such," rejoined the trapper.

To Sam and McVay the trader said, "You gents go help yourselves to some whiskey. I'll be there shortly."

"That's awful trustworthy of you, Buckskin."

"You been here before?"

Sam replied, "Couple of year ago; dropped a few dinero at your poker table." With a smile for Buckskin Williams he stepped after McVay, heading for the barroom hung on back of where drygoods and other items necessary to survival out here were sold.

In the barroom, McVay slouched down at a table as Sam went behind the log bar and hefted a bottle of corn whiskey. "These glasses are dust-rimmed, but I ain't all that fussy." He came around the bar and settled down where he had a clear view of the front doorway whilst McVay was sitting so's he could watch the back entrance.

"That bottle's marked."

"So it is," responded Sam as he smiled at the pencil markings the trader had made on the whiskey bottle. "No wonder he was so doggone trustworthy about letting us help ourselves."

"What do you think, I mean, about Mort Reiser

155

and even that gunslinger stopping here?"

"It's as good a starting place as any. What you've got out here"—Sam nodded out a window—"is the start of some awful rugged mountain country. There's places southeast of here where hosses are in high demand, Chico, Jardine, Cinnabar, to name a few mining camps. There ain't no railroad out thisaway or any roads to speak of. Just the mountains and I'm hoping those we're after."

"How you gents doing?"

"Tolerable." Sam figured Buckskin Williams had stepped outside to check the brands on their horses. And if Reiser and Mackley had overnighted at Benson's Landing, he was pretty certain both of them had left behind a general description of himself and his deputies.

"You heading for the mines?"

"Why we're here."

"How much do we owe you?"

The trader smiled at Joe McVay. "Just keep pouring them down."

"Right clever of you to mark this whiskey bottle."

"Have to, with the kind of clientele I've got."

"Now that's an educated word."

"You said you were here before?"

"Yup."

"Most who stop here never come back."

"Suppose they're just hoping to get a glimpse of civilization again."

The trader dropped a hand behind the bar when footsteps sounded on the wooden floor, and now Kiley Glover sauntered in and said, "This place is as quiet as a monastary. Give me two fingers around and a cold beer if'n you've got it."

"Just got whiskey," the trader said.

"What kept you, Kiley?"

"Why, Sam, you know my hoss's been ailing."

"I've got some for sale."

"It ain't like I've got to put that bronc out of its misery, gents." Glover sat down next to Sam Chapman. "Anyway, I hear hosses are damned expensive in these parts."

"Scarce as hen's teeth. Matter of fact, a waddy named Reiser brought some through about a week ago."

"Nope, that name don't ring a bell. But we did send a friend of ours ahead to check out some of these mining places . . . Bilo Mackley. Kind of dark skinned, hawkish face."

Buckskin Williams frowned, then he shook his head and mumbled, "That name don't register with me."

"Well, we might as well tally up," murmured Sam as he shoved up from the chair and took the one step to the bar.

"That'll be ten silver dollars."

"Awful steep."

"This is steep country, mister. Being you've been here before I should know your handle—"

"Sam Chapman to my friends."

"Chapman? Common enough name. But I don't recall. You boys stop back now."

The trader came around the bar and began swiping at the table as his customers passed through the main building and went outside to find their horses. Only when he heard them riding away did Buckskin Williams pass through the wide doorway and stalk toward the man sleeping off his drunk in that quiet corner. His boot nudged into Mack Turner's ribcage a couple of times before the man stopped snoring and managed to jerk his eyes open.

"That lawman Mort Reiser told us about just left."

"What lawman?" The outlaw groaned and closed his eyes.

"You never could hold your whiskey, Mack. But hangover or no, I want you to make tracks for Chico Hot Springs and tell Ojeda that Marshal Sam Chapman is heading his way. Dammit, Mack roust yourself . . . Or I'll really shove this boot into your mangy hide."

Chapter Fifteen

"Seems peaceful enough."

"More peaceful than Benson's Landing."

Sam glanced over at his deputies. "At least we didn't lay over at Benson's Landing and wind up with ticks or worse."

He lifted his eyes from the wooden ferry perched on this side of the Yellowstone to the massive mountain range eastward. In ravines lifting up mountainsides would be found the mining towns. They were about an hour away from where they'd nighted, the sun up but behind the crested peaks of the Absarokas. Dew still clung to buffalo grass and shone dully on the tangled serpent of underbrush marking a creek edging into the river. They were just downstream from this, under a gnarled cottonwood and still feeling the chill of night. Snow piebalded the higher elevations, the blacker bands sparse belts of trees, and Sam felt the shadowy hulk of the mountains seemed higher than they should be, just below the moving sky. A man either took to these heights or shied away, mused Sam Chapman.

"Beyond the river is a place called Chico. Not as big as other mining camps but just as hazardous to a man's health if he don't watch out."

159

"You don't have to wetnurse us, Marshal Chapman," muttered Kiley Glover.

"Just hope you wastrels were weaned properly. Let's go roust that ferryman out of his warm shack."

With Joe McVay spurring ahead and along a worn track, they rode out from under the trees and to the openness along the riverbank. McVay brought his horse up to the cabin door and leaned over some and hammered on the door. "Anybody home?" he yelled.

"I hear you!" came a muffled response. Moments later the door creaked open and an old white-haired man stepped outside. "Getting so a man can't even enjoy a morning's cup of coffee."

"We want to cross."

"Then swim them nags across. I've got bacon and eggs a-simmering on the stove and biscuits in the oven. Which means I ain't open 'til I've 'et."

"By jingles, Sam, that just set my stomach to growling somethin' fierce," said Glover.

"This ain't no restaurant!"

"Would a silver dollar buy us something to eat?"

"Out here that might buy a toothpick." He scratched an undecided hand across his scraggly white beard. "But you do have the earmarks of someone used to hard work. Come on then, tie up your horses, an' hustle in 'cause them vittles is about to burn up."

Somehow all four of them managed to wedge around a small square rickety table in a cramped kitchen filled with too much heat from the black cast-iron stove. But there were no complaints from men used to eating cold meals. Being the horses were tied just outside the near window, their nickering carried into the cabin, and then one of them whickered loudly, and another.

"Probably caught the scent of a grizzly; plenty of them black devils hereabouts."

"Probably," agreed Sam. "I suppose all those miners across the river are getting rich."

"More like a lot of them are barely holding on."

"Do traders bring many horses through here," Sam asked casually as he speared another couple of slabs of bacon and a biscuit.

"Most generally once or twice a week horses are trailed through here. You looking to buy some?"

"Could be."

The oldtimer squinted quizzly at Sam as he gummed some food around in his toothless mouth. "That 'could be' has a lot of meaning, mister. You're no miner, or shiftless cowpoke, or outlaw I figure. And if you're a starpacker, I figure you're too smart to wear your badge in these parts."

"Let's just say we're looking for some old friends."

A cackle narrowed the ferryman's blue-rheumy eyes. "I knew it . . . I can spot one of you lawmen a mile away. Old friends? Maybe it's someone I know?"

"I've heard these are Red Ojeda's stomping grounds."

"You've heard right. And that's all I've got to say about Ojeda. He's a mean one, is Ojeda, tolerable mean. Uses my ferry to fetch his horses across the Yellowstone. But I don't discuss him or his gang, just so Ojeda don't ventilate this tough old hide of mine."

161

Sam fingered out a couple of silver dollars and placed them next to his empty plate. "That was sure enough easy on the stomach."

"Hosses are acting up again," said McVay as he rose and went to open the door and stepped outside.

They walked their horses down to the ferry and brought them aboard just as the sun speared between two peaks and sent a lot of shadows scurrying away. Right away it seemed to warm up more, with Kiley Glover giving Sam one of his sly looks.

"He read you down to a T, Sam."

"How's that?" Sam shortened his grip on the reins as his bronc began quartering away.

"About you being used to honest labor."

Some of Sam's edgy mood went away, and he said jocularly, "I'd say he's a damned good judge of character." He managed to quiet his horse down as the sluggish craft moved out into the river. Perhaps, as that oldtimer had told them, the horses had picked up the scent of a bear. Nonetheless Sam studied the far bank of the Yellowstone and the rising land beyond. He strode over to Joe McVay standing next to Glover. "What do you make of it?"

McVay spoke first. "Like somebody's getting ready to lift my scalplock. I figure we got away from Benson Landing's too easy."

"Me too," agreed Sam.

"Come on," said Glover, "there ain't nothing the other side of the river but more brush and mountains . . . and that Chico town."

Barely had Kiley Glover uttered those skeptical words than the calm of early morning was shattered

162

by gunfire. Lead slugs began gouging into the timbered craft seeking those aboard it. A slug punched into the railing at Sam's elbow and drove wooden splinters into his forearm even as he ducked and pulled out his handgun. McVay had also drawn his weapon and was scanning the eastern side of the river. Spotting gunsmoke, he yelled this out and fired back.

"We can't stay here!" Sam yelled.

"Who is it?"

"Could be the Red Ojeda bunch, or even Mort Reiser for all I know. We'll have to go back." A bullet nicked at his Stetson. "Get aboard your hosses and follow me."

Sam Chapman kicked the back gate open, then he untied the reins and got into the saddle, and without hesitating spurred his mount past the open gate and into the swirling waters of the Yellowstone. He was followed by Glover and McVay as more bullets slammed into the ferry. Which served as a barrier between the ambushers and those in the water, as they urged their swimming horses toward the western shoreline. Struggling out of the water, their horses carried them past the log cabin and into screening trees, where they swung down and at the same time reached for their long guns. Only to have the sound of riflefire die away.

"Who else but Red Ojeda," muttered Kiley Glover.

"Figure that," said Sam. "But at least we know where that cowardly scum is."

"And he knows where we are too, Sam."

"Which means Mort Reiser has hooked up with

163

that bunch. Let's go look for a place to ford the river. Then we can work our way back and pick up the trail of those ambushers."

It took them about an hour to cross over to the eastern side of the river and then they were coming onto the heights overlooking the ferry crossing. Amongst spruce trees Sam found a couple of spent shell casings; a Henry, he mused. Just beyond him, Joe McVay dropped out of the saddle and studied where the ground had been chewed up by horses. He picked up a bony piece of branch and drew a circle around a hoof marking as Glover and Sam brought their horses over.

"Reiser had his hoss shod over at O'Fallon. That smithy had a habit of using nails with square heads. At least this marking shows that."

"Has to be Reiser."

"If I remember correctly, Chico lies about a mile beyond this bluff."

"They could be waiting for us along the way."

"By now they figure we're still riding west with our tails tucked between our legs."

"Mort Reiser knows different," snapped Glover.

"Reiser ain't runnin' this show. Red Ojeda, as I recall, is real arrogant, and a man craving the bright lights and all its sinful comforts." Sam began walking his horse out of the trees. "I figure we'll try Chico Hot Springs first."

"What about Bilo Mackley? Think he'll have come this way?"

"If Mackley struck down the Yellowstone instead

of heading elsewhere, Joe, he would have passed through Benson's Landing. Got a good feeling about Mackley; he's been through here. And maybe we won't find him at Chico, but if not, there's other mining camps farther on."

After coming around a bend in the narrow road crowded by the high sides of a pass, they found themselves riding toward the mining settlement of Chico sprawled along Emigrant Gulch situated on the east side of the Yellowstone River Valley. Farther to the north lay some buildings which Sam gestured at as he said, "That be that hotel and plunge I was telling you wastrels about. A nice place to sweat the kinks out of your body."

"You told me Ojeda was more interested in cards and whores."

"When I encountered Ojeda before it was at the hot springs. Being a creature of habit he might be there now. Only one way to find out."

"This day has sure passed quickly."

"Just consider, Kiley, you're still in one piece and be thankful for it."

"Sure enough, Joe."

Twilight was pressing back the remnants of day when they dismounted before the main hotel, and with Sam passing inside to inquire about Red Ojeda and others he carried readers on. His deputies were getting restless when Sam finally emerged from the hotel. He told them of Red Ojeda departing yesterday for Chico, that for another silver dollar the hotel clerk had revealed the gang leader having a girlfriend there.

"No sense heading over there now," deliberated

Sam. "I figure if we mosey over after dark and try some of the saloons we'll find our quarry."

"You mean Reiser?"

"Right now I have no quarrel with Red Ojeda. Later, after we get Reiser and Bilo Mackley, maybe we can just ride back this way for another go at them outlaws."

"What'll we do until night sets in?"

"Kiley, I believe I'm gonna treat you boys to a mineral bath. Had one before, and it sure enough cured what ailed me."

"You mean you ain't afraid of manual labor no more, Sam?"

"Now, reckon this mineral water won't cure everything."

"Chico's what, a couple of miles farther south?" speculated Glover. "We could get rooms there, or at this fancy hotel, Sam."

"We'll night here."

"What's that funny round building yonder?"

"That, Joe, is the plunge. Contains what is referred to in elegant circles as a swimming pool."

Grumpily McVay said, "I'll just be needing a hot bath. Went swimming once, down in Wyoming, almost tangled up with a water snake."

"After seeing your ugly face that poor snake probably died of fright."

"I don't know, Kiley, seems to me Mr. McVay would make some woman a fine husband if he got rid of some of that shaggy rug covering his head and shaved once in a while. Reckon, Joe, you can tend to our horses while I see about rooms."

"Them hosses make better company than you two

shysters. Just don't take all night in that fancy plunge."

One of the ironclad rules at Chico Hot Springs was that anybody using the plunge had to rent a bathing suit. In the past on those rare times Sam, or even Kiley Glover, had taken a dip in some creek or waterhole it had been in their red flannels. Glover had been on the verge of open rebellion, just flat out refusing to accompany Sam over to the plunge, when it happened, a bunch of women flooding out of a hotel room clad in vari-colored bathing suits, caps and parasols. In passing Kiley Glover all of them gave him bold eyes, which saw the eager deputy going back and plunking down a thin dime for a rental suit.

"You know they're women of the night, Kiley."

"They is women, Sam, which is all I care about. That Chicotown must be some wild, rambling place."

"Just a rough hole is about all. Now take Cinnabar, down the line a piece. Got itself a player piano imported all the way from Denver. How do I look?"

Glover couldn't help laughing at Sam Chapman admiring himself in the mirror in their hotel room. Sam's bathing suit fitted snugly to his large frame but was chopped off above the knees and had short sleeves. Reaching for his gunbelt, Sam buckled it around his waist.

"You'd better bring yours," he told Glover.

"Afraid of them women of the night?"

"Those wastrels tried for us by the Yellowstone. I

still got some splinters in my arm. Figure they just might try again; here or when we go down to Chico."

"Okay, but can I take it off when I avail myself of that plunge?"

"We'll take turns going in, Kiley."

They left the room and sauntered down the corridor, and with Glover saying, "You're awful cautious. But like you said, this is rough country. Mort Reiser, I figure he backshot poor old Chili. What kind of wild tale did he tell Ojeda about us badgepackers?"

"That they'd want to ambush us. You'd have to understand Mr. Red Ojeda. We got acquainted over aces and eights. Long time ago; yup, down at the Longhorn Saloon at Dodge. Ojeda was younger then, just feeling his oats, same's me. Only difference is Mr. Ojeda had a killing rep—about that long ago time he'd gunned down four men. Tallied more with the passage of time. Those who chanced to be around when Ojeda and his gang got to robbing places. Oh, Ojeda was fast awright. But look at Doc Holliday an' Wild Bill Hickok an', well, that Texas gunslinger Bill Longley. Big, robust men. Able to go-round with either fist or gun."

"Meaning Ojeda is somewhat on the scrawny side?"

"Stands five feet two inches in a new pair of Justins."

"Damn, Sam, that's powerful short."

"But Ojeda's got a thickset pair of shoulders. Only thing is, they taper down to a puny waist and a short pair of legs. And worse . . ."

"I got the feeling this won't be pleasant."

Sam planted a hand on Glover's shoulder. "A shorter way of looking at things. I figure Ojeda's awful pissed 'cause we're out here trampling on his territory."

"You know, Marshal Chapman, just about now I wish you'd let Judge Garth hang us wastrels." Kiley Glover brightened when the cobbled walkway finally brought them to one of the doors passing into a high-roofed building. The damp smell of water came at them, as did the curious glances of those availing themselves of the mineral waters in the large swimming pool. Spread around the outside of the pool and below the high roof were oaken tables and chairs.

Stepping to a table, Sam removed his gunbelt as he noted the many doors spread around the encircling walls of the wooden enclosure. As he eased into the shallower end of the pool, Glover began sauntering past a couple of women seated at a table. A smile curled up Sam's lips when one of the women made the bold suggestion to Kiley Glover that they return to her hotel room. But the deputy seemed to have eyes for another harlot sitting alone at a table and reading a book.

Sam muttered silently, "She's probably holding that book upside down. But that wastrel Glover ain't easing over there just to gain some booklearning." For a while Sam tried an awkward dogpaddle, the warm water soothing to his tired body and mind, and then, as he swung over onto his back and began floating into deeper water, one of the doors was ripped open, and one of the women screamed at the sight of a man brandishing a handgun.

The gunman fired at Kiley Glover swinging startled eyes that way. As the bullet scoured into the wall behind Glover, he grabbed the woman by the arm and forced her out of the chair and behind him, then Glover was drawing even as other doors sprang open and more gunhands swept in. Down in the pool, Sam Chapman had just started to lift out of the water when two of the gunmen fired, and he had no choice but to throw himself toward deeper water. He went under as bullets pitted the surface.

"Reiser!" yelled Glover as he dropped a table onto its side and dropped on his knees behind it. Then he fired at Mort Reiser hovering by one of the open doors. Over the rapid sound of gunfire resounded the screams of the women where they huddled by the tables.

"Get him!" shouted Reiser.

"What about the one in the water?"

"He ain't got a gun. Get that damned Kiley Glover first!"

As the gunmen began closing in, hope flared in Glover's eyes when he spotted Joe McVay ducking into the large building. When McVay's gun bucked, one of the gunhands staggered sideways and plummeted into the swimming pool. Down to his last bullet, Glover fired at Mort Reiser ducking behind a door.

Unnoticed was Sam Chapman pulling himself out of the pool and making a grab for his holstered gun. He yelled, "Awright, hombre, drop it!"

For a moment the gunhand hesitated, then he realized the odds had been evened up, and along with Mort Reiser, he brought up his arms. But another simply turned and dove through a closed window, splintering glass. Suddenly it was over, the lawmen relieving Mort Reiser and the other hard-case of their weapons.

"You're hit, Kiley."

"Just caught a piece of my side. So, Mort, you couldn't turn away from your lawless ways."

"You were just lucky, damn you."

Kiley Glover backhanded the scowling Reiser across the face. "Sam, what say we hang this backshooter from one of those rafters."

"Just give him back his gun," McVay said flatly. "And me and him'll go for it."

"Nope," said Sam. "We hang Reiser without benefit of a trial it won't speak highly for the badges we carry. Cinnabar has a new jail. We can lodge these wastrels there until we catch up with Bilo Mackley. Then herd all of them back to Miles City."

"It was me, Mort," said Glover, "I'd end it right here."

"Tell me," broke in Sam, "did you boys catch a glimpse of Bilo Mackley?"

"Mister, I don't know no Mackley. Even if I did, I wouldn't speak of it to no lawman."

"You must have seen him, Reiser?"

"Just clap the irons on me, Chapman."

Around a shrugging smile Sam leathered his handgun. And almost in the same motion he drove a fist into Mort Reiser's midriff. Doubling up, Reiser grunted in pain and surprise, only to have Sam grab a hunk of hair and pull the man erect. "I know you saw Bilo Mackley. Either here or back

171

yonder at Benson's Landing." He sent a straight right hand slamming into Reiser's face, followed that with a wicked left jab, stood there as Reiser plummeted backward into the swimming pool. When Reiser broke surface sputtering and casting frightened eyes at the dead gunman floating facedown just a short distance away, he shied away from blood staining the water.

"Maybe winging Reiser might make him talk." In one smooth motion McVay brought up his sixgun and pulled the trigger. The lead slug tore the upper part of Reiser's ear away.

"No . . . no more," he screamed. "Yeah, I saw Mackley. It was back at Benson's Landing. Then he headed for . . . for Cinnabar or maybe Cooke City."

"That right?" Sam said to the other gunhand.

"He called it," the man said sullenly. "You may have us, Marshal Chapman, but don't count on it being for too long."

"Just long enough so you and Reiser stretch rope. Get irons on this wastrel, Kiley. Come on, Reiser, out of the pool."

After they had taken their prisoners over to the hotel and locked them manacled in a storage room, Marshal Chapman and his deputies returned to their rooms. Worrying Sam was the fact one of the gunhands had managed to get away. Right about now the man was back at Chico reporting to Red Ojeda. Though he carried a warrant for Ojeda's arrest, Sam realized the three of them would be no match against others riding with the gunfighter.

"How many you figure is riding with Ojeda?"

"Dozen or so, Kiley. Other than us there isn't

much law out here."

"Cinnabar should have a town marshal—"

"It does. Just the one man and no deputies. Hanging Reiser is mighty tempting, boys."

"To get to Cinnabar we have to pass through Chico."

"That's the short way. Longer is heading south along the Yellowstone. Which is the way we'll be moseying. There's one other thing, Kiley, Joe. And I know you boys have your hearts set on eating a hot meal here and enjoying them featherdusters."

"Doggonit, Sam, I need a break from all that riding," protested Glover.

"Within an hour or so I expect Red Ojeda to come a-calling. Not a social call either."

"Sam's right," McVay said. "The sooner we get moving the better chance we have of making it to Cinnabar."

"Yup," groaned Kiley Glover, "once I had me a golden opportunity to join the U.S. cavalry. At least there I'd get three squares a day and a warm place to sleep at night."

"I owe you one, Kiley."

"Reckon you do, Sam, but I've a hunch before this is over there'll be a lot more times like this. And those gals down at that plunge—all of them just dying to get their hands on me. Okay, I'm coming, Sam. Sorrowful as it makes me."

Chapter Sixteen

Under a moonless sky the hardcase brought his horse past a tent saloon pouring out light. On the way in to Chico he'd taken time to stop at a waterhole and wash drying blood away from the cut on his right cheekbone. He hadn't expected to go through that window, but what really set his teeth on edge was that other deputy showing up just when they had Marshal Chapman boxed in. Purcell was dead; Mort Reiser and Wortham placed under arrest.

"Of all the damnable luck."

The hardcase urged his horse around a freight wagon just rounding a corner and toward the hitch rail in front of Joe Ferguson's Sundown Saloon. He wasn't looking forward to telling Red Ojeda what had happened. First they'd had bad luck when those lawmen managed to get off that ferry and make it to the western back of the river. Then it had been Mort Reiser who insisted they wait as Marshal Chapman wasn't the kind to turn back. By tomorrow morning everyone in Chico and other mining camps would know that the Ojeda gang had come out second best in a sixgun showdown. The next thing to happen would be one of the camps organizing a vigilante committee. This wouldn't set well with gunfighter Ojeda either.

A large gambling room had just been added on to the saloon, but it was in an upstairs room that the hardcase expected to find Ojeda. Shouldering the door open, he took a hard right toward the crowded bar, drawn there by the need for some whiskey and the presence of another gang member.

"Run into some trouble, Murdock?"

"Yeah, dammit," the hardcase muttered angrily.

"That's a nasty cut."

Murdock retorted, "It'll heal. Where's Ojeda?" He grabbed the whiskey bottle and brought it to his lips.

"Was upstairs most of the afternoon. Right now Ojeda's back playing poker. Where are the others?"

"Suppose I tell you what happened, then you break the news to Ojeda."

"No way, Murdock. Me and Ojeda barely get along as it is. Well, what did happen?"

"Just trail along and you'll find out." Murdock elbowed another man out of the way as he turned away from the bar and headed back to the new gambling room. He was a hard man, had been an outlaw ever since he was fourteen and a member of Cantrell's Raiders. Drifting west, he'd robbed a few banks before hooking up with the Ojeda gang. Now in his late twenties, killing came naturally to Ty Murdock. Up here in Montana they'd run roughshod over small ranchers, and even taken on some of the bigger spreads, the cattle and horses they had rustled winding up in the hands of miners and unscrupulous stock buyers.

176

Passing through an open doorway, Murdock pulled up short when he spotted Ojeda dealing out some cards. Hovering at the outlaw's elbow was a darkhaired whore, one of those who worked here at the Sundown Saloon. Daytimes would generally find her waiting on customers. She was a tall woman, kind of full in the face with big red lips and jaded eyes, maybe more woman than Red Ojeda could handle. But tell that to the banty gunfighter and it would be the same as signing your death warrant. Though it galled him, Ty Murdock knew that he was afraid of Ojeda. That same feeling, he knew, was shared by the other hardcases. A vague smile flickered in his eyes when he noticed that sitting, the gunfighter seemed on an equal height with the other cardplayers, and only because Ojeda had put a cushion on his chair. From the table top up it seemed Ojeda was bigger than life with that large head of his covered with flowing brown locks spilling over the shoulders of his buckskin shirt. You could drink for a week out of that oversized tan Stetson. It was the eyes which revealed Ojeda's true character, being a pale blue and having a sort of cruel glint to them. Though his face would twist into contempt or anger or scorn, no change of expression ever showed in those eyes, and maybe this was what gave Red Ojeda the edge. All Murdock knew was that he hated to have them rest upon himself for any length of time.

Finishing the deal, Red Ojeda looked at the hardcase as he placed the deck aside and picked up his hand. "You're back," he grunted in a disinterested tone of voice.

"Red, can we talk privately?"

"Trouble?" Ojeda tossed in a couple of blue chips while smiling at the other players. "Maybe my luck's changing."

Murdock returned the whore's cold look as he leaned over and whispered in Ojeda's ear. "We got more than we bargained for." Quickly, nervously, he narrated just what had happened over at Chico Hot Springs.

Viciously Ojeda said, "You were supposed to take them out by the river."

"Tried that first."

"Damn," the gunfighter muttered bitterly. "Just when my luck turned good, this has to happen. That'll be all for me, gents."

The gunfighter brought his men over to where they settled around a back table. Mostly the saloon had miners crowding into both the barroom and back here, but in evidence were gamblers and a few hardeyed men. As yet Chico hadn't gotten around to electing a town marshal. And this was the way Ojeda wanted it. Though a few highwayman and petty thiefs preyed on the miners, up until now the Ojeda gang had been content to rustle cattle and horses. As for the miners, these hardy men didn't care where their beef or horses came from, treated Ojeda more as a protector than a threat.

"This is the first time," Ojeda rasped, "that a U.S. marshal had the gall to head out thisaway."

"Chapman was just damned lucky."

"Luck has nothing to do with it. Times are changing. Rustling is getting to be a dangerous game. Both the lawmen and ranchers are learning

178

where our favorite hideouts are, and the trails we use to bring livestock out here. It's just a matter of time until there's a shootout. What I'm saying is we need to turn our eyes elsewhere."

"Robbing a few miners won't do it."

"But there's gold shipments. Out of Cinnabar and Cooke City. And there's that meddler, Marshal Chapman. I figure he won't give up until he finds Bilo Mackley. Only thing is, we're gonna find Chapman first. We head out at first light for Chico Hot Springs."

They were two days out of Lame Deer and making good time around the northern reaches of the Big Horns. And they'd only come this way because Tonto Blair had insisted on it. More and more it was becoming clear to Sheriff Toby Pindale that he wasn't in charge of this manhunt, and it rankled him. Back at Lame Deer, the Crow Indian agent had practically ordered them off the reservation, when all they were looking for was a guide. The one they'd taken on, a Crow going by the name of Black Eagle, claimed to know that mountainous land west of the Big Horns.

Pindale was getting a little saddle-weary, and it showed in the way he rode along with that irritated set to his blocky face. By the sun he figured it was midafternoon. Ever since leaving Lame Deer their guide had kept up a fast pace, with Pindale's objecting to this overruled by Tonto Blair. Perhaps it would have been better, he mused, if Blair and that other gunhand had gone after Bilo Mackley and left him behind at Miles City.

A day later the party of three white men and the Crow scout were cutting westward across the Big Horn Basin. They followed yet another river, the North Fork of the Shoshone, through a light rainfall. Closer were the rugged peaks of the Absarokas, but there the sky was clear, with snow still piebalding these heights. Along the way they had spotted small bunches of cattle and a few pronghorns, and once a cowhand swinging away to break over a distant elevation. Their guide, Black Eagle, had told them it was possible they might encounter roving bands of Indians, some of those who'd refused to come in to the reservations, Sioux or even Cheyenne.

Toby Pindale was thinking about this as rainwater began seeping under the collar of his yellow slicker. This only served to make him surlier, and he muttered. "The safer way would have been to head west along the Yellowstone."

Tonto Blair eyed him for a moment before replying, "Out here there isn't any safe way. You don't like it, sheriff, just turn tail for Miles City."

This was what Sheriff Pindale wanted to do. By doing so, however, it would tell the folks back there he wasn't fit to be their sheriff. And there was Judge Garth. He'd been chewing on it ever since leaving Miles City, the way the judge had taken this special interest in Bilo Mackley. Pindale was of the opinion that whatever the judge's reasons for keeping hired guns on the Clearwater payroll was for legal purposes. Though a lot of people had valid reason to mistrust Judge Garth, the U.S. government thought differently when it appointed him to the federal bench. That was good enough for Toby Pindale. But what he was still puzzling over was Judge Garth giving a ne'er-do-well like Sam Chapman that marshal's job. It would have been a feather in Pindale's cap if he would have been appointed. Chapman, he figured, knew less about the law than either of his deputies, that it would be only a matter of time, maybe weeks at the most, before Sam Chapman proved he wasn't fit to be a lawman, and a tight smile rode across Pindale's wide mouth.

Which was swept away by the unexpected reappearance of Black Eagle. The Crow had ridden on ahead to check out an open stretch of prairie. Coming in, Black Eagle barely slowed his paint horse as he shouted gutterally, "Hunkpapa Sioux . . . just over that rise."

In a remarkable display of horsemanship, Black Eagle swung his horse toward the beckoning river, and even before the others could take after him, he'd swept below the embankment.

The cracking of a rifle as several horsemen pounded over a rocky elevation almost dislodged Sheriff Pindale from his saddle. He managed to grab the saddlehorn, his gaping eyes taking in a ragged line of renegade Sioux, before he realized that Tonto Blair and the other gunhand, Rico Calder, had left him behind. Frantically he spurred his gelding toward the riverbank, with lead slugs plunking into the ground behind him. He came down the muddy bank to find the others swimming their horses toward a small island littered with

181

swaying trees and dense underbrush. Without hesitating Pindale plunged his horse out into the sluggish current. Again he almost came out of the saddle, clung to it as his horse went after the others. In his fear of the moment Pindale had forgotten to unsheath his rifle to keep it dry, though he found the Smith & Wesson in his right hand.

"Damn, what'll happen next?"

Pindale's horse touched bottom, then began struggling through fetlock-deep mud even as Tonto Blair and Calder and the Crow scout were returning the fire of at least a dozen Sioux warriors pulling up along the riverbank. When one sagged in the saddle, and another toppled out of his, the renegade Sioux swung away and vanished.

"Hell, Pindale," jeered Rico Calder, "Your face is the color of a dirty cloud."

"Just didn't expect this to happen," gasped Toby Pindale as he slid down from his horse. He walked it over and tied it next to Blair's gray bronc.

Tonto Blair spoke from where he had settled behind a fallen cottonwood. "I expect they'll keep us pinned down until sundown. Be worried if there was more of them. Tough hombres, these Sioux, so they might try to rush us. Rico, go up thataway a piece and settle in. Those Sioux could cross the river and hit us from the north. So, Black Eagle, keep an eye out that way."

"What about me?"

"You can start building a campfire, Pindale. It'll be noon a-fore long."

"The Indian could do that," protested Toby Pindale.

"Do it," the gunfighter said coldly.

Despite his fear of the man, Pindale said, "Let's clear the air as to who's in charge here. I hired you on as my deputy, not to . . ."

"The judge hired me. To find Bilo Mackley. You're tagging along just to make it look legallike. You got that?"

Sheriff Toby Pindale wilted under Blair's unyielding gaze.

"Once you get that fire going, rustle up some grub and coffee." There was still in Tonto Blair this overpowering urge to force the sheriff into drawing on him. Whether Pindale went down here or after they found Bilo Mackley was one and the same to him.

By the middle of the afternoon it had warmed into the high eighties, and there was no wind to drive away the mosquitos pestering both men and horses. The fire Pindale had made had gone out. While the sheriff had taken up position further east along the island perhaps an acre in size. Ever since that first sighting, the Sioux hadn't tried to come in again. In Toby Pindale was this hope that they'd headed out someplace. Meanwhile, his hatred for Tonto Blair was keeping his mind occupied. That Blair held him in open contempt was all too obvious. But what could he do, up and fire the man? Blair must have struck some deal with Judge Garth, meaning that his role as a sheriff was simply to lend support to the others.

"When I get back to Miles City, there's gonna be a showdown with the judge."

None too soon for those lurking on the river

island, the sun began sinking beneath the jagged peaks westward. Still they waited until there were no more shadows fringing down from the screening trees, until the sky was heavy with stars. Someplace close at hand an owl let go with a nervewracking screech, which brought Pindale thumbing back the hammer on his handgun. One of the horses kicked at another, then quieted down. Rico Calder came ghosting in through the underbrush to hunker by Blair, who said, "I'm beginning to believe those Indians took off after easier prey."

"Maybe so. What do you figure on doing, nighting here?"

"Nope. Go call in that scout. I want to make tracks away from here."

Rico Calder hurried on foot through the underbrush, and when he came back several minutes later it was to tell his companions that Black Eagle was gone. "Those Hunkpapa Sioux spooked him out of here."

"Well, he's gone. Damn him." Tonto Blair untied his reins from a tree branch and sought the saddle. "About the only thing we can do now is cut west and work our way around those mountains. That damned Crow told me of another way over them, but chancing it was too risky. Come on, let's ride."

"I'm telling you the truth, Mr. Ojeda, I don't know where that U.S. marshal went."

The gunfighter lashed out with the barrel of his .45 Peacemaker and cut the man's cheek open to the bone. "You're lying! Dammit, old man, my patience is running thin."

"Please," gasped the ferryman as he sagged onto a chair, "That marshal didn't come through here last night, or this morning."

"What do you think, Red?"

Ojeda shoved the old man away and strode to the open door. "We know he left that hotel at Chico Hot Springs. That he didn't come south through Chico. But I feel it in my bones that marshal is heading south, probably along the river, with Mort Reiser and Wortham. Yup, heading for Cinnabar."

"We'd best ride then."

"Not before we burn this place down." He frowned at the big cast-iron stove. "That thing's too hot to fool with. Murdock, go get your hoss and we'll have us some fun."

After the gunhand had ridden his horse close to the open front door of the log shack, an order from Ojeda brought his lasso whipping in, which Ojeda snaked around the stove, and with the near end wrapped around Murdock's saddlehorn. At Ojeda's let-her-rip, Murdock spurred his horse away from the front porch to topple the stove and its burning contents onto the wooden floor. Ojeda came out laughing followed by the terrified man who ran the ferry. Eagerly flames were eating at the dry wood as the outlaws claimed their horses.

"What about him?"

Spurring his horse into a lope, Ojeda called back to the gunhand, "Kill him."

As the others headed south along the riverband, the outlaw, a rail-thin Kansan known only as Rappadon, unlimbered his long gun and a nasty smile for the old man making a break for his ferry. He waited until the ferryman was almost there, then he triggered his rifle. The slug caught the old man high in the left shoulder and spun him around, where he dropped to his knees to take the next bullet squarely in the chest. He toppled bellydown as the outlaw broke out whistling as he swung away.

Chapter Seventeen

In weather typical for this high plateau country, light, driving snow followed the lawmen into Cinnabar. It wasn't heavy enough to erase their view of Devil's Slide, a name given to the red-streaked vertical dikes lancing down the face of Cinnabar Mountain. An inquiry by Sam Chapman of a passing freighter brought them deeper into the mining town where they reined up before a long building set off by itself. To ward off the unseasonal chill they'd donned rain slickers. But Mort Reiser didn't have one or a coat, and the testy hardcase was only too glad to be helped off his horse and escorted into the city jail, a boxlike and dreary structure with one window facing south.

"This place ain't got no office for the town marshal, just these two cells," lamented Kiley Glover. "But there's the key for them."

"Should I get a fire going in that stove?"

"You might, since I don't want Reiser to catch his death of cold. I'll go pay my respects to the town marshal. That being over at the Cactus Saloon."

"Wait up and I'll join you," stated Glover as he placed the ring of keys back on the wall peg.

"Joe, we'll stable your horse. Meet us at the saloon."

Once the horses had been tended to, Sam and Kiley Glover emerged from the livery stable into glaring sunlight. It had stopped snowing, with the formless clouds pressing low upon the mountain being shredded away. As Sam expected, he found town marshal Kurt Heinzel occupying one of the chairs at a poker table in the Cactus Saloon. Sam's only venture through Cinnabar had been a couple of summers ago, that as a drifting gambler, and the off-chance he might be able to stake a claim. At the time the founders of Cinnabar were convinced the red streaks in nearby Devil's Slide were pure cinnabar. Only it hadn't been mercuric sulphide ore, just the extension of coal veins sunken underground. Others had come in to mine the coal and also to build coke ovens. Through all of this a lot of miners went after placer gold, but in Sam Chapman's opinion backbreaking work like this would soon wither a man away.

"Some corn whiskey sounds good, Kiley. I'm buying."

They bought a bottle at the crowded bar and found an empty table. On that previous visit, which lasted a little over two weeks, Sam had been one of the regulars at the standard Sunday horse races. The town had three saloons, a lot of log cabins and tents and a winding main street with deep ruts crisscrossing it. Supplies were freighted in at considerable expense.

In Sam's eyes at the moment was a speculative glimmer for his table companion. Back where they'd recrossed the Yellowstone River the swirling rapids had frightened Mort Reiser's bronc, and when it bucked Reiser out of the saddle, Sam reacted quickly.

"Hiyee!" yelled Sam Chapman as he forced his horse to the left and toward Reiser just bobbing to the surface.

Then Sam was plunging out of the saddle. Desperately he swam downstream as the current brought him around seeking boulders where he managed to grab Reiser's shirt while yelling.

"Joe, unlimber that rope of yours!"

Even as he spoke Mort Reiser was struggling to get out of Sam's grasp. There was stark unreasoning fear in Reiser's eyes, and Sam knew the man didn't know what he was doing, and to save both of their lives, the clenched fist he unleashed rendered the man he'd just saved unconscious. The next moment Joe McVay's riata splashed across the foamy waters and across Sam's arms. He made a grab for it, draped the wide loop around both of them. When the riata went taut it jerked those in the water away from a dropoff and toward the riverbank.

It was here they set up camp. And here, too, he could see the questioning looks on the faces of his fellow lawmen. Staring off into the settling darkness to gather his thoughts, Glover finally said, "I doubt if I would have saved Reiser."

"Goes for me too, Sam."

"Expect he'll hang when we bring him back to Miles City," threw in Sam. "With those irons around his wrists Reiser would'a drowned. Would have felt

189

real bad if'n I hadn't done something. Or it could be, you wastrels, aging had something to do with it."

Refilling his shot glass, Sam Chapman let the memory of what had happened back at the Yellowstone filter away. But replacing it were other words spoken by Kiley Glover in that Glover wanted to stop looking for Bilo Mackley, a sentiment echoed by McVay back at that lonely campfire.

"I reckon being a lawman has its drawbacks, Kiley. Especially when you consider I forced you into wearing a badge."

"It ain't all that, Sam. For all we know Mackley could be down in Wyoming by now, or other places farther south."

"He could."

"We've got Reiser and that other one, Wortham. But as I recall, didn't Judge Garth order you not to go looking for Bilo Mackley?"

"What I'm afraid of, Kiley, is that when Sheriff Toby Pindale catches up with Mackley, there'll be no trial."

"You figure Pindale'll just gun him down? Toby Pindale . . . I don't think he's got the stomach for something like that."

"It sure as hell isn't Pindale I'm worried about."

"You mean Tonto Blair then?"

"Yup, Blair. Without Bilo Mackley around to testify against him, Judge Harlan A. Garth will get away with murder. I won't like that a-tall."

"The judge is a sly one," muttered Glover as indecision danced in his eyes.

"And there's what Mackley did to Mag Burns

190

. . . to one of her girls. I want Mackley, bad. Not just for what he did to Mag. But to see that Garth gets the same justice he's been handing out to others. McVay'll be here soon." Sam shoved up from the chair. "Talk this over with McVay. But whatever you wastrels decide, it was an honor riding with you."

With a pleasant smile for Kiley Glover, Sam weaved through the crowd to where the town marshal of Cinnabar was playing poker. He watched a few hands being played while resisting the urge to get into the game. A couple of times the curious eyes of Kurt Heinzel took in the newcomer. Heinzel was one of those big, blocky men, with farmer's hands and a wide face. When he played Heinzel had a habit of tugging at his full beard, this before asking for more cards or when anteing. Finally he looked Sam Chapman full in the face and inquired, "Chapman, wasn't it?"

"Been a spell, Marshal Heinzel."

"The lure of gold dust bring you back?"

"Some law work."

"That a fact?" Heinzel said quietly. "Watch my chips, Burt." He came erect and followed Sam to a front window. "Someone steal your horse?"

Sam brought out the U.S. marshal's badge, gave Heinzel a brief glimpse before pocketing it again. "I lodged a couple of prisoners in your jail."

"Anyone from around here?"

"Couple of those riding with Red Ojeda."

"Red's tolerable mean," commented Kurt Heinzel in a dry aside. "What charges you got against these boys?"

191

"Mort Reiser is wanted for murder. As for the other one, Wortham, just about the same charge."

"Humph. Just how did a gambling drifter like yourself get to wearing a badge—"

"I got to thinking I was a Republican."

Heinzel allowed a quick smile to appear. "Notions of that sort can get a man into a passel of trouble. What about Ojeda, the rest of his bunch?"

"The truth is I came thisaway hunting Reiser. Seems he joined Ojeda's gang. In a shootout over at Chico Hot Springs we downed one, arrested the others."

"Then you're not alone?"

"Got a couple of deputy marshals. And I'd consider it a favor, Kurt, if I could lodge my prisoners in your jail for a few days." Reaching into an inner coat pocket, Sam took out the reader he had on Bilo Mackley, and on which county clerk Otis Plumb had made a charcoal drawing of the wanted gunhand.

"Mackley . . . yup, came through a short time ago. As a matter of fact he took me and the boys yonder for a hundred or so. Drifted on."

"Any idea where?"

Heinzel scratched vigorously at his dark brown beard. "Yup, I do believe Mackley rode eastward. That would take him to Silver Gate, or beyond to Cooke City. As for your prisoners, marshal, I'd have to charge for their keep."

"Would a government pay voucher suffice?"

"It would. Tell you what, Chapman, when you get back we'll settle up. Now, as you've just arrived, I'd sure admire to have supper with another lawman. Your deputies are invited too."

In a somewhat worried tone of voice Sam replied, "Guess they might have other plans, Kurt. But right about now a steak would sure hit the spot."

At first Sam Chapman wasn't certain what had brought him out of a restless sleep. Perhaps it was sleeping in a feather bed after the cold nights he'd spent in his sleeping bag, and with only the hard ground for a mattress. He tried dozing off again. Only to toss the blanket aside after a few minutes and get out of bed. The heavy snoring of Kurt Heinzel came at him from across the room in a boarding house one block removed from the main street. A stride to the only window showed a vague light just beginning to tint the eastern sky, and by his reckonings another two hours until sunup.

After dining last night with the marshal of Cinnabar, they'd gone back to the Cactus Saloon, to while away a few hours before calling it a night. His deputies hadn't been there, and Sam figured they found more action in one of the other saloons or just wanted to get off by themselves and talk things over. At least, he mused, they could have stopped by and given him their decision. In a way he felt slighted.

"Kept them wastrels from stretching rope." Then a regretful aside. "But I got Chili Tugwell gunned down. Sure enough out here life's a calculated risk."

He dressed quickly in the chilly room. For it was Sam's intention to leave without rousing Heinzel or, once he'd claimed his horse, avoid any curious eyes.

Briefly there was a desire to shave off a week's growth of stubbly beard. That would mean heating water and having to light a lamp, and he discarded the notion as he picked up his weathered hat and eased out of the room.

He found the livery stable without any difficulty, and his bronc in one of the rear stalls. And a lantern hanging from a beam, to which he touched flame. Once the bronc realized it was Sam snaking the saddle blanket over its broad back it went back to chomping hay.

"We're heading out early, hoss. Be another tough day with me in the saddle you just waiting to hump your back and try bucking me off when my guard is down." He reached under the bronc's belly for the double saddle cinches. Tightening them, he spoke again in that low monotone, "So I figure a truce is in order—me not stretching it into a gallop, and you, hoss, just a-keeping it gentle."

Then Sam spun away from the bronc and made a stab for his Smith & Wesson when clumps of hay suddenly dropped on him from above, this and the dry crackling of a gun being hammered back.

"Damn, Sam," came a familiar voice, "I didn't know you liked to talk to hosses."

"Kiley," he barked up at the opening in the floor above, and at Glover and Joe McVay grinning down at him. "You sports almost got ventilated."

"You hightailing it, Marshal Chapman?"

Scowling, he spat out, "Appears that way." The scowl soon gave away to an easy grin as he holstered his handgun.

"We figured as much," said McVay. "Reason we

194

bunked down up here."

"Yup, we couldn't afford no room like you Republicans. Such is the lot of the common man."

"Sam, it didn't seem right and proper us not going after Bilo Mackley too."

"That your final word on the matter?"

"It be that, awright."

"Then get cracking down here and saddled up. It just could be that Ojeda has some friends hereabouts. So's I want to leave before any of them are stirring."

"Maybe we've seen the last of Ojeda—"

"Don't be getting careless about that, Kiley. Out here us lawmen are outcasts in a wicked world. Reason we didn't come in here wearing our badges, nor when we get to Silver Gate and beyond. Out here tinny little badges make tempting targets."

Kiley Glover came down the wall ladder first and remarked as he stepped past Sam, "Yup, but ain't they pretty."

"Reason you"—Sam led his bronc out of the stall—"decided to tag along?"

"Well, you did keep us from getting hung. That counts for something. Another reason is you wear on a man, Sam, you truly do. So who else but Joe and me'll traipse with you over these damnable mountains just to hear your particular brand of malarky. Every day I learn me some new words."

"Well, Mr. Kiley Glover," responded Sam, "how's about you learning another one—disrespect. Trouble with you wastrels is that your folks never belted your backsides with some willow branches when you got sassy."

As his deputies walked their horses to the back door and opened it, Sam blew out the lantern. Climbing into the saddle, Sam rode outside and drew up between Glover and McVay. Then he brought them behind the buildings on main street. There was a brief glimpse of the jail, and it was then that Sam had this sudden feeling that something was wrong. He debated with the idea of turning around and looking in on his prisoners, discarded it when someone appeared between two buildings on main street. Spurring his horse into a lope, Sam set his sights and mind on the southeasterly running trail and the man he was after, Bilo Mackley.

Chapter Eighteen

The town marshal of Cinnabar wasn't at all surprised to find that his guest for the night had left. And upon arising, Kurt Heinzel had gone over to Broderick's Cafe to have his usual morning cup of coffee and breakfast of side pork and gravy. There he'd found the newly elected mayor of Cinnabar and T.C. Blackwell, a member of the city council and the owner of a dry goods store. As Heinzel anticipated, they inquired about his prisoners.

"A U.S. marshal brought them in."

"It's our understanding these men ride with Red Ojeda."

"Then in my opinion, this U.S. marshal should remove these prisoners from our jail and take them to Red Lodge."

"Afraid Marshal Chapman left town."

"That's damned impertinent of him."

"This worries me, Blackwell, knowing Ojeda's reputation."

"I'm the one stands to get hurt if Ojeda comes here. The least you could do is give me a deputy."

"Dammit, Kurt, you're working parttime as it is.

We . . . we just don't have the money."

Heinzel shoved his cup away and rose. "There's been talk of forming a vigilante committee. Something I'd welcome."

"About those prisoners, we're not expected to feed them."

"We'll see they don't starve to death. Get paid for it when Marshal Chapman gets back."

"If Chapman ever gets back."

Kurt Heinzel was still grumbling when he let the door slam behind him and plodded downstreet. The sun came at his back, low and unblemished by cloud cover. Dew still glistened on the few patches of grass and sagebrush growing amongst the scattered buildings making up the town. Later, when he'd started a fire in the jail stove and tended to the prisoners, Heinzel planned to work on his claim a few miles south of town, along a creek curling down out of the mountain. Once in a while he'd find a few nuggets, but lately he had it in mind to pull out of here and try his luck over by Silver Gate.

As Heinzel turned the corner onto an empty lot, he was surprised to see a miner he knew hurrying his way toting a Sharps rifle, and with the man blurting out, "Had to warn you, Kurt. There's some longriders breaking into your jail."

"Ojeda!" he muttered. "Come on." Heinzel unleathered his old Dragoon as his stride quickened.

They passed another building, a log cabin pouring out chimney smoke, and hurried beyond that to draw up by a pole corral, where they watched Ojeda coming out of the jail behind the two men

198

he'd released from their cells.

"Far enough, Ojeda!"

"Well, if it ain't the esteemed marshal of Cinnabar." A brazen hand signal from the outlaw caused his men to rein their horses to either side in an attempt to box the marshal in by the corral. "Maybe we could make a deal, Heinzel?"

The miner said, "I don't trust no longrider."

"Seems we got no choice. Unless you feel like swapping lead with Ojeda and ten other men." Standing there, Heinzel realized it was too late to make a break for the log house, but more cuttingly, to expect any help from the townspeople. "I hear you, Ojeda."

"I expect Marshal Chapman told you where he was heading?"

"He did," replied Heinzel as he choked down his anger. By telling the gunfighter, he'd be a part of Marshal Chapman getting killed. But unlike the town marshal of Cinnabar, Chapman had a couple of deputy marshals, and anyway, what choice did he have. "Eastward. Heading eastward for Silver Gate . . . least Chapman told me that."

"Fair enough."

"What about my prisoners?"

"They'll be riding with me." Ojeda waited until Mort Reiser and Wortham were mounted on the spare horses he'd brought along, then lithely Ojeda found his own saddle. He threw Heinzel a last, lingering smile before wheeling and loping away without a backward glance. The other hardcases held their horses to the gait set by Ojeda.

While back at the corral Kurt Heinzel slammed

199

an angry hand down at a pole. Even thinking of getting a posse together would be out of the question. For once those outlaws were gone, those eking out a living here would soon forget what had just happened. Daily in these parts were killings, petty thievery, with highwaymen lurking along the trails stringing the mining camps together.

"That was damned brazen of Ojeda."

"Could have forced the issue. But not on what they're paying me. Tell me, Shorty, you interested in buying my claim?"

They were coming deeper into the mountains, and along a rutted track used by freighters and the Overland stagecoach. East of Red Ojeda and the other outlaws stretched a bench, a flat elevated reach of land edging onto foothills beyond which soared the Absarokas. Sometimes along creeks they glimpsed the shacks or tents of those looking for gold. Mostly they beheld the spruce forest of the mountains thinning out at timberline where jagged peaks gnawed at the sky.

As he rode, Red Ojeda had been trying to draw out Mort Reiser about what had been happening back at Miles City. In an uncharacteristic gesture Ojeda offered the man riding alongside him a cigar. "Enjoy it, Reiser, as a good smoke is hard to find in these parts.

"Obliged, Red," grinned Mort Reiser. "And for breaking us out of that calaboose. Now I just want to line my sights on Marshal Sam Chapman."

"My sentiments," echoed Ojeda. The gunfighter

seemed to joggle in the saddle more than others, or because of his short stature it just appeared that way. Behind him and Reiser the others rode in pairs while chatting, though a few sat their saddles in cantering silence.

"Why all these questions about Miles City?"

"Reasons," Ojeda said vaguely.

But what Red Ojeda hadn't told any of the others that it was because a Judge Harlan A. Garth he'd spent time in the Montana Territorial Prison. A man can find out a lot of things while serving time, from the longtimers and those just being brought in. And there were some on the verge of being released from prison, such a man being Bilo Mackley. Later on he'd found out that Mackley had been hired on at the Clearwater Ranch, out of Miles City. Much to his surprise he learned that Judge Garth owned the Clearwater. What gnawed at Ojeda was the reason for a judge having known gunhands on his payroll. Upon being released from prison, Ojeda swung westward to piece a gang together and get back into the rustling game. All the while, though, there was in Red Ojeda the notion that someday he would even the score with Judge Garth. Then to Ojeda's surprise there appeared at Benson's Landing gunhand Bilo Mackley.

A couple of Ojeda's men held their guns on Mackley as they brought him into Buckskin Williams's trading post and back to the bar where the gangleader, Ojeda, was holding court. One of the hardcases sneered, "Look who we caught trying to sneak across the river."

"I'll be skinned, if it ain't my old cellmate, Bilo Mackley," Ojeda motioned toward a chair. "Give Bilo back his guns."

With a hard look for those who'd gotten the drop on him, Mackley shoved the hideout gun into an inner coat pocket, and leathered the sixgun before easing across the rickety table from Red Ojeda. His trousers and boots were still wet from when he'd forded the river. About him was this sullen manner, while the hard riding Bilo Mackley had done lately had gotten rid of the slight paunch. "Thanks, Red, for calling off your dogs."

"Least I could do." He crooked a finger. "Buckskin, fetch a glass for my friend here, Bilo. Only one thing could bring you to these parts, Bilo, and that's law trouble."

"You always did have an inquisitive nature."

"Reason I'm still alive. Last I heard, you were working at the Clearwater."

Surprise flickered in Mackley's hard blue eyes.

And Ojeda added, "Working for Judge Garth."

"I was," Mackley said bitterly. "Never thought Garth would turn on me, especially after what me and him done." A couple of glasses of corn liquor served to make Mackley more talkative. Then one more brought out the telling of how he helped Judge Garth take out the owner of the Clearwater Ranch, an elderly westerner named George Davine. "Buried his body someplace along the Tongue River. Afterward Garth used some legal means to acquire the Clearwater."

"That's been a few years ago, Bilo. Kind of strange the judge would turn on you now."

"Something else happened," snapped Bilo Mackley.

When Red Ojeda exhaled a cloud of cigar smoke it brought him away from that chance meeting at Benson's Landing to him joggling in the saddle alongside Mort Reiser. Ojeda wasn't one for spending long days in the saddle, and now he swung his eyes westward to the afternoon sun, gauged it to be going on five at least. Sensing Ojeda's mood, one of the outlaws called out, "Red, I spotted some white-tailed deer sulking in that draw. Would be nice to have venison for a change."

"Go for it. We'll camp up ahead by that creek meandering through them birch trees. Always did like the way moonlight came down through those trees; sparkling kind of silvery."

And that evening the moon appeared seemingly in response to the gunfighter's request, to beam down upon a large campfire and the outlaws gorging themselves on venison. Whiskey was plentiful, with only Ojeda not drinking. He motioned Mort Reiser away from the others and to the creek bank, the cigar clenched between Ojeda's bony-white teeth glowing as he inhaled smoke.

This was about what he'd learned so far from Reiser about Marshal Sam Chapman. That Chapman had made Miles City his personal stomping grounds. Somehow the man had sided with the Republicans in this last election, and as a reward Chapman now wore a U.S. marshal's badge. But Red Ojeda felt it was more than Chapman being appointed a lawman. The man behind all of this, of course, was Judge Garth. Why would the judge send Chapman all the way out here especially since the U.S. marshal at Bozeman was responsible for this part of territorial Montana. To Ojeda it could only mean that Marshal Chapman had orders not to bring Bilo Mackley, but to gun the man down.

Which brought Ojeda's thoughts centering on Mackley. A few years back Ojeda had it in mind to bushwhack Judge Garth. The reason being the judge had doublecrossed him when Ojeda had delivered some rustled cattle out to the fringes of the Clearwater. Instead of paying him the agreed on amount, Ojeda had been arrested by that stooge of Garth's, Sheriff Toby Pindale and a small army of deputies. Now just killing Judge Garth had lost some of its bittersweet flavor. Now what Red Ojeda wanted was for the very law the judge claimed he supported to work against the man. This was where Bilo Mackley came in. For hadn't Mackley more or less confessed when they'd encountered one another at Benson's Landing his part in the killing of that rancher. Mackley had clamped the lid down tight on his present troubles. And now Ojeda's eyes slid questioningly to Mort Reiser sucking on a whiskey bottle.

"What kind of trouble has Mackley gotten himself into now, Mort?"

Lowering the bottle, Reiser said in a voice tight with whiskey, "A hard hombre, is Mackley. Could be any kind."

"He sure as hell didn't wrangle cattle out at the Clearwater."

"Nope. Hung around with the judge's son, Rye."

"Yeah, I remember Rye Garth. A real spoiled

204

sonofabitch if I recall. Heard Rye liked his cards and women."

"You betcha he did. Rye could be found at a lot of places along the Yellowstone. Had a wild temper. Lucky them hardcases was along to keep a lot of gents from piling and hammering him."

Red Ojeda dragged on his cigar as he lifted contented eyes to moonlight seeping through the birch trees in sort of silvery waves because of the slight breeze stirring the branches. He truly enjoyed this owlhooter's life, killing when it needed being done, taking what belonged to others, but mostly the uncertainties of this hard existence. Just being a part of it was more of an aphrodisiac than gambling or women. He would match his draw against any man's, Hickok's, Earp's, Bill Longley's. What he wasn't was a forgiving man. Nor did Red Ojeda have a shred of conscience. He swung his mind back to Mackley.

News traveled fast along the Yellowstone Basin. So it was old news to Ojeda, those whores being killed. Was it possible, mused the gunfighter, as his probing eyes turned to Reiser again, these killings could be tied in to Bilo Mackley? Or even Rye Garth.

"You say Rye Garth spent more time gambling and chasing women than out at the Clearwater—"

"He had the money to do it."

"Now, Mort, you was a deputy marshal. As such, maybe you know who's been killing these whores?"

"Just bar talk is all I've heard."

"That'll do for starters."

Frowning, Reiser inquired, "Why this sudden interest in these gals . . . and Rye Garth?"

"I'm making it my business to find out all I can about this," Ojeda said flintily. "So what about this bar talk?"

"Just that it seems awful funny to a lot of folks, Rye Garth being around when something of that nature happens. Rye and Mackley and those other hardcases."

It struck Red Ojeda then, almost as if he'd just downed a whole glass of rotgut whiskey, that this was the connection he'd been seeking. Somehow Rye Garth was mixed up in these killings . . . the judge trying to protect his son . . . Bilo Mackley cutting out for the gold camps. Now more than ever he wanted to keep Mackley alive. Which meant getting to Marshal Chapman before Chapman could do his killing for Judge Garth. There was the afterward, when he had Bilo Mackley. Somehow he would get Mackley to Bozeman where the man would confess to that U.S. marshal.

"Judge Garth, you're going down, you damned doublecrosser."

"What's that, Red?"

"Just the wind rattling my teeth. It'll be a hard ride tomorrow, Mort, you others, so peel out them bedrolls."

"You still figure on goin' after that Marshal Chapman?"

"Him and someone else. Now hit them bedrolls."

Chapter Nineteen

Back about ten miles an encounter with some miners revealed this was Soda Butte Creek. That this ribbon of trail meandering alongside the creek was the main route to the mining towns of Silver Gate and Cooke City. They were deeper in the mountains now, Sam Chapman and his pair of deputy marshals. Every so often their eyes would go eastward to Granite peak, which Sam had heard was the highest mountain in Montana, and a part of the Beartooth Range. Once a lone horseman had viewed them from a craggy elevation. Probably a highwayman, Glover had remarked at the time, Which brought home to the lawmen their reasons for being out in this high plateau country.

Soda Butte Creek was located in a wide valley flowing west to east. There was plenty of timber, which would give cover to game animals or anyone lurking close at hand. Their horses moved easily in the heat of day, and every so often they'd break into a canter, but at the moment a hand signal from Sam brought them to a halt as he nodded ahead.

"That must be Silver Gate."

"Kind of a sprawling place."

"Not as big as Cooke City. Got the usual run of

low dives and gambling joints. Along with Odie Madison's Imperial Casino."

"Now that sure sounds impressive."

"Quite the place, Kiley. Big place; about half a city block. Got a balcony running around the second floor and that high ceiling. Yup, Odie Madison is a big thinker. Where most of the gambling action takes place."

"You mentioned Bilo Mackley liking to gamble."

"If Mackley's out here at all, it'll be at Silver Gate, or possibly Cooke City. One other thing . . ."

"You gonna tell us wastrels to behave?" said Joe McVay.

"This time when we ride into Silver Gate, it'll be as bonafide lawmen. Pin 'em on, boys." Sam dug out his badge and pinned it to his woolen shirt. "Next you wastrels better check the loads in your sixguns. 'Cause those who don't, tend to worry about that and a heap of other things once lead gets to zipping around their ears."

"Somehow I get the feeling Mackley isn't far away."

He squinted over at Glover. "I'm beginning to itch some. Now I know none of my ex-wives are hereabouts. So that could only mean one thing."

They found Silver Gate to be spread out on both sides of the creek, a lot of random buildings, tents, corrals, outhouses, and more crowded than when Sam had passed through before. He brought them at a walk past a Chinese laundry and along a narrow lane toward a corral hooked to a livery stable. Three men sat out front on a wooden bench, one whittling, the others chatting away until Sam's badge caught a tracery of sunlight. After that all three idlers paid close attention when the lawmen swung down, with Sam breaking into a smile.

"Gentlemen, a fine day."

The whittler found his voice. "That badge for real?"

"Marshal Sam Chapman at your service, gents. You the hostler?"

"Uh . . . yup, I is, marshal. Any special reason you're here in Silver Gate?"

"Could be. Any room in there for our hosses?"

"Pick out your stalls. Charge is two bits a day, per horse."

"I hope that includes some sweet feed."

"Bin's inside; help yourself to the feed, too."

Inside the livery stable, they removed the saddle rigging from their horses and rubbed them down. When they emerged from the stable only the hostler sat out front. Striding down the lane, Sam remarked, "I guess it does pay to advertise."

"You mean our wearing our badges?"

"By noon everyone here will know a U.S. marshal is in town. Meaning that if Bilo Mackley is hereabouts, learning that we're here could spook him out of his hiding place. Or he just might be over at yonder casino." Sam nodded at the largest building on the next street.

"If Mackley's at the Imperial, I doubt he'll give up without a fight."

"So I guess it's about time we earned our pay, Sam."

"It is. You two come in the back door. There's a lot of people in town today. So I expect the Imperial will be crowded. That could work to our advantage in us getting the drop on Mackley. I'll go in the front door. Just want you boys to back up my play."

While his deputies crossed the narrow street, Sam angled down it. He didn't seem to attract any attention amongst others dressed as he was. A lot of miners were about, a few women, while passing wagons slithered through muddy ruts due to last night's light rainfall. Sam slipped once to have a boot drop into a deep rut, but on yonder boardwalk he stomped the mud away and sought the batwings of the Imperial Casino.

The barroom and where the gambling took place was one large room. Back of this a red velvet curtain decorated a wide stage, with steps running down to either side so the girls who pranced upon it could go down and mingle with the customers. A balcony encircled the action below and support beams jutted up to the galvanized ceiling. For being midday, the place was crowded. Over to one side a photographer, this being Cyril Aleyard of Civil War fame, was about to take a picture of two miners posing at a table, while a dog kept trying to leap into one of the miner's laps. The bardogs were nattied up in starched shirts, string ties, and vests. Flitting amongst the tables were barmaids whilst at an upright piano a seedy-looking drummer kept banging out his rendition of "Give the Fiddler a Dram."

Sam noted all of this and the fact there were some who matched Mackley's general description. Last he'd seen Bilo Mackley, and this at a distance, the man had on rough garb, worn Levi's and a black leather vest over a black shirt. Sam eased slowly past the front windows, and since he was taller than most, his presence was noted right away.

"Mackley, yonder at that table," he remarked silently. But a Bilo Mackley wearing black broadcloth and white linen and fancy trousers, and a black low-crowned hat. And mused Sam, a man enjoying the wages of sin. The man he was after sat with his back to Sam, who let his eyes flick for the briefest of moments to Glover and McVay emerging from a back hallway and moving apart as they sauntered up through the crowded tables.

When Sam Chapman eased up behind Mackley, he nodded at some of the players eyeing him back while palming his Smith & Wesson and nudging the barrel against Mackley's neck, to have the man stiffen.

"Easy, Bilo, I'm trail-weary and this gun has a hair-trigger."

"Who the hell . . ."

"Man's wearing a badge, Mackley," warned one of the players as he eased his chair away from the table, to have others do the same.

"Pindale, you've got a hell of a nerve," blustered Mackley, "bracing me out here."

"It ain't Sheriff Toby Pindale," muttered Sam, and he reached down and lifted the gunhand's sixgun out of its holster. "It's U.S. Marshal Sam Chapman. Those other two are my deputies."

"Damn you, Chapman. You can't get away . . ."

Sam pulled the gunhand out of the chair and spun the man around, and he spat out angrily, "I'm finding it damned hard to forget what you did to Mag Burns and one of her girls, Mackley." He took out a pair of handcuffs and snapped them around Bilo Mackley's wrist.

"Thank you for doing that, marshal!"

Swiveling that way, Sam gazed in open surprise at Sheriff Toby Pindale standing alongside Tonto Blair and another hardcase, and with their handguns covering not only Sam but his deputy marshals.

"Speak of the devil, and he shows up. Sorry, Pindale, but this man is my prisoner."

"Not any more," Pindale said loudly.

It was now that Sam noticed the din of moments ago had melted into suspenseful silence. That it was his gun against three more. And more importantly, if he turned Mackley over to these men, Mackley would never be brought back to Miles City.

He said, "I turn Mackley over to you, Pindale, all you'll do is kill him! Everyone here hear that. This other wastrel is Tonto Blair, a no-account gunfighter. No, Pindale, you'd better make your move right about now."

An Overland stagecoach clattered past Red Ojeda dismounting in front of a tent saloon. Others belonging to the gang brought their horses farther upstreet. Ojeda had told them to be on the lookout for Bilo Mackley and that marshal, Sam Chapman. While just to Ojeda's right stood Mort Reiser eyeing a rifle behind the display window of a mercantile store.

"A nice weapon, Red."

"Any weapon is nice if it can kill someone."

There was still in Ojeda a lot of distrust for the man from Miles City, Reiser. He had Reiser pegged as not being overly bright, a man too lazy for honest work and just not up to robbing banks or holding up stagecoaches. It could be, if the opportunity presented itself, Reiser would backshoot him, pondered the gunfighter, the same as he'd done to Chili Tugwell. He hadn't detailed to Reiser their reasons for being here, and it would be interesting to see if Reiser would use that hogleg of his when they did accost Marshal Chapman. Reiser's hands would probably be shaking so much the man would blow away his own kneecap just trying to unleather that sixgun. Then he told Mort Reiser they were going to check out the Imperial Casino.

"Heard of that place," Reiser said off-handedly. He was full of self-importance because Ojeda had singled him out. Hitching at his gunbelt, he paused along with Ojeda as a freight wagon rumbled by. "The first drink's on me, Red."

But the gunfighter only grunted when he stepped up onto the boardwalk and entered the Imperial. He took in everything at a glance — the way people were edged against the walls — the three men holding their weapons on Marshal Chapman — and Bilo Mackley standing there with manacles on his wrists. What surprised Ojeda most of all was Chapman telling these men of their intentions to take Mackley someplace and then gun him down. It was then that Red Ojeda saw the badge pinned to the shirt of Toby Pindale.

"Yup, dammit," he muttered softly, bitterly, "it's Judge Garth's hatchet man, Sheriff Pindale. An' I owe that bastard plenty for what he done."

Mort Reiser said hoarsely, "That's Chapman and . . . and Pindale?"

"Yeah," Ojeda said disdainfully, "you're a bright one, Reiser. Guess who else is here—Tonto Blair."

"The gunfighter?"

"Knew I'd run into Tonto again." Ojeda began flexing the fingers of his right hand to limber them up. "Back my play, Reiser."

Said Mort Reiser in a quaking voice, "Su . . . re . . . sure."

"Marshal Chapman," Ojeda called out, "I'm backing your play."

It was Sheriff Toby Pindale who swung around first, and with Tonto Blair pivoting just slightly so he could keep an eye on Sam Chapman and the newcomers. Deputy Marshals Glover and McVay saw their chance as they drew their weapons but held back from firing. Just a short distance away the man of Civil War fame, Cyril Aleyard, lifted his tripoded camera around, Aleyard's bespectacled eyes filled with the excitement of the moment, and seemingly a disdain for danger. He was about to take a photograph, out here more commonly known as mirrors of memory, which would become famous throughout the West as the shootout at the Imperial Casino between gunfighters Red Ojeda and Tonto Blair and Marshal Sam Chapman. Quickly he ducked under the light-tight cloth, sensed that violence was about to break out, and squeezed the black bulb that tripped the camera which simultaneously exploded the gunpowder on his lighting apparatus, the mini-ball of light startling everyone there.

Tonto Blair swung on Ojeda, only to have the slug from his handgun slam into the chest of Mort Reiser. The other hardcase next to Blair swung down on Sam, whose own Smith & Wesson barked a split-second sooner, and the hardcase staggered sideways and went tripping over an errant chair. Now it was Tonto Blair grabbing Sheriff Toby Pindale, using the man for a shield as he backed toward a side window even as he fired again at Red Ojeda.

Unmindful of Pindale shielding Tonto Blair, Ojeda fanned the trigger on his big Peacemaker. The first slug punched a hole in the frightened sheriff's left hand, the second and third dotting into Pindale's pale white shirt about chest high. Then Tonto Blair was thrusting the dying sheriff of Miles City away and throwing himself through the window. A couple of Red Ojeda bullets punched out after Blair.

Suddenly it was over, but it took a couple of uneasy heartbeats for those still in the Imperial Casino to let that fact register. All of the worthies in the gunfight still had firm grips on their weapons, and with Ojeda half-turning to note the presence of those riding with him. He glared through lifting gunsmoke at U.S. Marshal Chapman.

"So we meet again, Chapman."

"Why the sudden interest in my welfare?"

"I came here to kill you, Chapman."

"Figured that."

"Because I had it figured you came out here to

gun down Bilo Mackley. Then I heard what you said to Pindale."

"Just why do you want to keep Mackley, here, alive?"

Red Ojeda holstered his gun. "It was my intentions to turn Mackley over to the U.S. marshal up at Bozeman."

"I find that hard to believe, coming from a longrider like you, Ojeda."

"Let's just say I owe Judge Harlan A. Garth a favor. Meaning that it's pay-back time for what Garth did to me a few years back."

"Glad to meet another admirer of Garth's."

"Now I figure you and your deputies, Chapman, can get Mackley back to Miles City so's he can testify against Garth."

"I intend doing that." Sam grinned. "You know, Red, I've got a reader on you."

"So?"

"Maybe the next go-around I'll come looking for you."

"It'll be something to look forward to, Chapman. Meanwhile, I don't think you've heard the last of Tonto Blair. Blair's got a rep for finishing what he starts, come hell or high water."

"Obliged you told me that."

"Well, Marshal Chapman, you've got a long ride in front of you."

"You planning to stick around Silver Gate?"

"Could be, or I just might mosey back to Chico. *Hasta luego.*"

"For this old hoss it's *hasta la vista,* Ojeda."

Chapter Twenty

This was their second day out of Cooke City, and by now Sam was convinced the plainsman knew his way through the Beartooth Range. Back at Cooke City, it was with some disappointment Sam learned this was the end of the line for the Overland Stagecoach Company. So instead of making that long trek back to the Yellowstone River and follow it around to Miles City, Sam and his deputies had decided to hire on Zach Lankford. Lankford was a grizzled old plainsman, somewhat blocky, with black sunken eyes and a shaggy gray-streaked beard, and clad in buckskin.

Along with the pack animal, there was Bilo Mackley snugged down on a gelding. Upon finding out they would trek over the mountains, the gunhand had voiced his opinion in no uncertain terms. A rap alongside the head from Kiley Glover had put an end to that nonsense. As for the plainsman, he'd been hired on to guide them only because of a shared acquaintance with Sam of a rancher named Moses Quinta. Sam had run into Quinta, a reformed gunfighter, several years ago down in Colorado. That Quinta was married and residing in the

Big Horn Basin was another surprise.

With an eye for the cloud-shrouded mountains, Sam looked over at Zach Lankford slouched on a rangy bay, a horse having a white star marking its forehead and surefooted when it came to rugged terrain. "I just hope that Quinta is luckier at marriage than me."

"Doing all right married to this Celia gal. But both man and woman are two stubborn critters." The moaning wind riffled Lankford's longish gray hair under the worn and befeathered hat. "How does it feel being a lawman?"

"Sometimes like I'm going through a long losing streak at poker."

"Know the feeling, Sam." Lankford squinted into the distance. "Yup, there's a grizzle on the prowl down in that valley. Lots of them rascals out here. At times they give fair warning; more often not."

"You've got Tonto Blair on your mind, Zach."

"Blair's no one to mess with. But from what you told me he got his comeuppance back at Silver Gate. Should be the last you'll see of him."

"He was paid to come out here and gun down my prisoner. According to Red Ojeda, and he should know, Tonto Blair isn't done with us."

"It's been two days, Sam, and I've scouted out our backtrail. Came up with nothing. Either he ain't back there or Tonto Blair's better at this tracking game than I figured."

Slicing across the way they were heading was Muddy Creek, one of many streams passing down from farther up in the mountains. Mostly there were steep valleys hidden below the peaks, a wild

218

place marked only by game trails or ribbons of water. It was Lankford's opinion they could make Red Lodge in a week, and from there catch a stagecoach to Miles City. But Sam realized it might take longer to get through these uncharted heights, for the horses were just getting broken in to scaling ravines and struggling up from valley floors. Coming at them in the heat of a sunny afternoon was a piney scent, and flowers adorned meadows as did wild grasses and mountain birds.

"I could see how a man would want to stay up here."

"Pretty now," rasped Lankford. "Hell come winter."

"You're a wanderer like me."

"Only kind of life appeals to me, Marshal Chapman."

When it was closing on nightfall, Zach Lankford brought them onto the shore of a large lake. Enclosing them in were stately pine trees, and they swung down to set about making camp under the trees with the lowering sun spilling golden rays upon the rippling and clear lake waters. Beyond them and northward, Lankford had pointed out, lay Beartooth Butte. Quartering around them were the lofty peaks of the Beartooths. As Sam brought his prisoner off the horse, he watched Lankford melt away into the trees, knew the plainsman was heading back the way they'd just traveled to see if they were being followed.

Sam removed the handcuff from Bilo Mackley's left wrist, and after making the man hunker down with his back against a slender fir tree, he said, "Awright, Mackley, put both hands behind you."

"Where can I get to in this forsaken hole?" protested the hardcase.

"What I'm seeking tonight is peace of mind." Sam snapped the handcuff back on the man's left wrist as a resigned sigh passed through Mackley's lips. "If you wanna go wandering off, Bilo, you'll have to take that tree with you."

"You're really gonna take me back to Miles City?"

"Yup."

His bitter laughter rippled up through the branches. "Might as well do me in right here, Chapman. Once I'm back there, the judge'll make damned sure I don't testify in court."

"Would you rather we leave you here so's Tonto Blair can pump you full of holes."

"There ain't nobody following us, Chapman!"

"For your sake I hope not."

"What's that supposed to mean?"

"Heard that Tonto Blair is a finisher, Bilo. Judge Garth hired Tonto to kill you."

"You're the one wearing the badge," blustered Mackley.

Sam smiled and replied, "But you're the one can send the judge to prison."

While Sam had been talking to Mackley, his deputies had gotten a fire going. Now Sam strode past their campfire to his horse, which he unsaddled, along with Mackley's. By the time he had brought his saddle and bedroll closer to the campfire, there were only fiery traces of the lowering sun to the west and shadows embraced the pine forest of the mountain. Higher up on the peaks it was brighter, and as yet no stars had appeared. Even now they could feel a chill creeping in. Almost an hour later the ghostly reappearance of Zach Lankford brought questioning eyes to the plainsman.

As was his habit, Lankford tended to his horse first. Then he settled down by the others, and where Kiley Glover handed him a cup of piping hot coffee and a tin plate holding a supper of makeshift beef stew. After Lankford had taken a tentative mouthful of stew, he cast a squinting eye upon Glover just to his left.

"Won't die from it."

"Guess that'll do."

In a more serious tone of voice Lankford said, "Came across fresh tracks back there; a lone rider. Lost the trail north of here. Figure whoever it is passed near Beartooth Butte." He set worried eyes on Sam. "You figure it's Tonto Blair?"

"Can't figure otherwise."

"Tomorrow we'll be passing through some open country as we come onto a chain of lakes. If it's this gunfighter, that's where he'll hit us."

"Tell you what," Glover said with a nod toward Bilo Mackley, "we could send him on ahead."

"That could solve our problems," agreed Joe McVay.

"What do you say, Mackley?"

The gunhand stared back at Sam Chapman. "Wouldn't surprise me none you sending me out there unarmed."

"Seems everyone," retorted Sam, "wants a piece of your mangy hide."

"Well," spoke up Lankford, "I could scalp and geld him for you. But there's still someone out there a-waiting for us."

"Any other way through these mountains?"

"Where we're heading is about the only way, Sam. Least we forget there's more of us than him. What did you call this, Mr. Glover, beef stew?"

"Want another helping?"

Zach Lankford allowed a pleased grin to splash across his mouth. "Yup, and some more coffee. Tell you what, Kiley, your cooking is about equal to that of a Blackfoot squaw I knew once upon a long ago time. Her specialty being roasted dog—not a few pieces of meat but the whole dog, insides and all. Tasty as all get out. Just speak up if you want her recipe. Although, this stew here has about the same flavor."

Kiley Glover couldn't help but break out laughing. "I do consider that a compliment, Mr. Lankford."

In the morning, well before first light, they rose to find that a light coating of snow had dusted the ground and covered trees. A hurried fire was made, then some coffee washed down with cold biscuits. Once snow had been kicked over the fire, they set out along Beartooth Lake. Under different circumstances the lawmen would have enjoyed traipsing through high plateau country charted only by the Indian or mountain man. For the worry of what lay ahead showed in the nervous flicking of their eyes and that nobody tried striking up a conversation. But something else seemed to be bothering Kiley Glover, in the way he kept drifting glances over at

222

Bilo Mackley slouched aboard his horse. It wasn't until they cleared the lake and were following Zach Lankford bringing them through timberland that Glover spurred to catch up with Sam Chapman.

"Tell me, who does Tonto Blair want to take out—"

"Mackley?"

"Chew on this, Sam. Back at Silver Gate it was noted by Tonto Blair that Mackley was dressed damned fancy."

"That fancy garb of Mackley's is sure rumpled now though."

"I want to switch clothes with Mackley. Him getting back to Miles City is what this is all about."

"Kiley, you could be signing your death warrant."

"Chance I'm willing to take."

Around a quick smile Sam said, "You've changed some."

"Just earning my pay, Marshal Chapman. Mackley's about my size. Besides, I always did have a hankering to wear a fancy getup like that."

"Zach," Sam called out, "Hold up." Then he swung his horse around and rode back to Bilo Mackley sitting his bronc just in front of Joe McVay. He fished out his keys to have a tracery of fear widen Mackley's eyes.

"What's this all about?"

"You and my deputy are gonna change clothes."

"It's damned cold out here," protested Mackley.

"Tonto Blair will be sighting in on the gent wearing those clothes, Mackley. You can either suffer a little chill or wait until a hot slug tears into your innards."

Once the two men had changed clothing, and Bilo Mackley was handcuffed and aboard his horse, the horsemen set out into the spreading light of early morning. The timber was giving way to more open country. A short time later Lankford jerked a thumb toward an elk breaking for a stand of pine trees. But as he rode, Lankford, those just behind, kept their eyes sighted ahead to the crowns of trees and rocky crags in the hopes that blue jays or other mountain birds would take wing to warn them of possible danger. Around midmorning they splashed across Little Bear Creek, with their loping horses leaving it behind. Without warning, a mule deer burst over a rise and upon sighting these mounted intruders swung to the south and bounded away, and then it happened, the heavy reverberating of a rifle — Kiley Glover grunting in pain and crumpling over his saddle — his comrades holding onto their reins as they dropped out of their saddles and sought what shelter there was. For Sam Chapman that was behind his bronc, while Joe McVay swung his horse and Mackley's toward a small copse of firs, and with the plainsman yelling testily, "Seems it came from up thataway!"

The rifle crackled again, and this time it was Kiley Glover's horse that caught the slug meant for its rider. The bronc whickered in agony as its forelegs buckled, throwing Glover to the ground. Then Sam and Zach Lankford were firing their long guns at a tree-littered precipice about a quarter of a mile to the north, their slugs chipping away bits of stone before ricocheting away. It was Lankford who finally said, "I reckon we scared him

224

off."

Sam nodded as he pivoted away and hurried over to kneel down by Kiley Glover. He grimaced at the blood staining Glover's left shoulder, and from Glover he received a hazy smile. "Sam, you were right about a man running into a lot of bad luck if he wore fancy garb like this."

"Got you in the shoulder, Kiley."

"Just plug it up and let's get after that damned ambusher."

"Aim to do that," said Sam as he helped Glover to his feet, then he walked him over to the trees and made Glover sit down. "Kiley, here's the way of it. We're going after Tonto Blair. That means you'll have to watch Mackley."

"No sweat."

This time Sam brought his prisoner over and made him stand facing a limber pine, his arms around it and the handcuffs secured again to his wrists. Zach Lankford had come up, and he said, "This snow's melting fast. But it'll help us find Tonto. There's a string of lakes just ahead, boys, stretching northwesterly. A lot of timber around them, and along with the man we're after there'll probably be grizzlies. Ever tracked a man a-fore?"

"Nope," said Joe McVay, "but man or bear, I'm gonna nail that sonofabitch."

"Kiley," said Sam as he unbuckled a saddlebag flap and pulled out a small bottle of corn whiskey, "this'll help ease the pain. It's warming up fast, could get into the fifties by noon."

"Don't fret none about me," grimaced Kiley Glover. "I've busted a bone or two before, and the

225

way this shoulder feels that slug must have passed on through. One other thing, don't any of you wastrels get gunned down by that no-account. Now get a-riding before Tonto Blair makes it to China."

Staring down at delicate pink stars and other flowers, alpine forgot-me-nots and elegant camas, decorating a small meadow, Sam wondered how so much beauty could exist in a place of sudden violence. About an hour ago they had found the rocky elevation where Tonto Blair had lurked in ambush. Tracks leading from there had brought them closer to the chain of lakes mentioned by Zach Lankford. They were spread out but riding abreast, with Lankford in the middle and guiding on the vague hoof markings left by Tonto Blair's horse. Around them burned out timber caused by a recent fire stood in skeletal silence, though new growth covered the grassy terrain. Just off to their right an occasional opening in the trees let them glimpse one of the lakes.

While the man they were after, Tonto Blair, was a couple of miles farther north. For a while he had ridden along a small lake, and now Blair had urged his horse through aspens and to a height which would give him a view of those trailing him.

"Come on, dammit," he cursed as his bronc started to whicker and resist the gunfighter's reined command to go on up the tree-speckled slope. On the way through here he'd spotted a few bear, but in the far distance, while the last thing on Tonto Blair's mind at the moment was an encounter with one of them. He lashed his reins down at the horse's shoulder and spurred viciously, to have the bronc labor upslope.

As the slope leveled off, Tonto Blair took a minute to gaze at the nearby peaks of the Beartooths. He had no particular liking for these mountains, or any heights for that matter, but it was Blair's arrogant way of doing things. The truth was he hated to be rushed by any man, respected no one, least of all Judge Harlan A. Garth. What kept him heading after Bilo Mackley was a fierce pride, that he was a man of his word.

"Told that damnfool judge I'd kill Mackley. Well, the job is done. Now when these fools come calling, it'll just be some more notches on my gun."

Lost in his own prideful reveries, Tonto Blair didn't seem to notice that his bronc was still trembling, not from the hard ride nor climb, but that it had caught the scent of a silvertip grizzly. "Stop that fussing around," he said crossly as he swung down and tied the reins to a tree branch. He pulled out his Winchester and stole ahead to find a place to settle in and wait for those lawmen.

As he waited, the rifle stacked against a mossy-green boulder and the warming sun beaming down through firs, Tonto Blair took out the makings. He had made it a long habit of only smoking three handrolleds a day. Nimbly his supple fingers rolled a cigarette into shape, with his thoughts drifting back to Miles City. What Blair had in mind to do was to go back and get Mackley's body. From there he planned to take it back and present it to the judge.

"That old bastard might not take my word about Mackley being dead."

Another fifteen minutes passed before he caught sight of a horseman leaving the shelter of some pines and veering toward the lake shore. A short while later another rider appeared, then a third. They were still out of rifle range, perhaps three miles to the southeast. And when they picked up Blair's trail, he allowed a frosty smile to touch his cold eyes.

He reached for his rifle and checked its action before placing it carefully before him on the flat top of the boulder. Still he waited, waited until they were out in the open more and no more'n five hundred yards from where he lurked. At this range, and as they got closer, Tonto Blair knew that he couldn't miss. He would take the one riding closer to the timber first, the plainsman next, then Marshal Chapman riding closer to the lake. Now he nestled the stock against his stubbled cheek and crooked a finger around the trigger, one eye sighting down the long barrel, the other kind of smiling coldly. And then the unexpected happened.

The first thing Tonto Blair heard was the ghastly and enraged roar of a silvertip, next shrubbery being torn aside even as he tried swinging around. He tried to rise, to bring his Winchester to bear on a large grizzly looming over him, only to have the grizzly come in with crunching teeth and raking fore-claws. Though his gun sounded, and he might have hit the silvertip, Tonto Blair screamed in pain when the grizzly clamped its teeth onto his shoulder, the raking claws gouging at his torso. He tried swinging away, with one hand vainly seeking his holstered sixgun as they grappled near the high dropoff. Somehow he fell backward, with the grizzly still on him, and then both man and bear were toppling over the high ledge. They struck far below, and only then did they fall apart.

The lawmen and Zach Lankford had watched in horrified surprise all that had happened. Now they rode on and soon found Tonto Blair's mutilated body, and the grizzly breathing its last. There was no remorse in Sam's eyes, nor the others, and with Sam saying after a while, "Glad it was him."

"He deserved it."

"His horse, probably left it up there." Joe McVay swung away. "I'll go get it."

"Do that," muttered Sam Chapman, "Then we'd best head back and tend to Kiley. Expect he's really hurting about now."

Zach Lankford swung after Marshal Chapman. "He had us dead to rights."

"About time a little luck came our way."

"Yup, but unlucky for Tonto Blair it snowed."

"The way of it, Zach, the luck of the draw."

Chapter Twenty-one

Sam Chapman took a last lingering look at the Beartooths before climbing into the stagecoach. Settling down across from his deputies and Bilo Mackley seated between them, he smiled at Zach Lankford.

"Couldn't have made it without you, Zach."

"Shucks, Marshal Chapman, it were a pleasure."

"Where are you heading now?"

"With the money you gave me, well, I hear things are hell-roaring over at Butte because of copper being discovered."

"You're no miner," chided Sam.

"But there's a lot of girlies and action over there."

"Guess you're more like me than I thought. Take care, Zach."

And Sam grasped the plainsman's hand as the driver of the stagecoach shouted they were leaving Red Lodge. That climb over the mountains had played their horses out, and rather than keeping them, Sam had sold them to a horse trader. Using the money to pay for Lankford's services and tickets for himself and the others. Here at Red Lodge he'd also sent a telegram to a citizen of Miles City requesting that the man meet them at Big Timber. He hadn't told his deputies about sending that wire. As the stage cleared Red Lodge and rolled northward, he gazed fondly at Kiley Glover and Joe McVay. They had proved out. Gone was that cynical attitude of theirs, to be replaced by an inner confidence and sureness of manner.

"Judge Harlan A. Garth," Sam mused silently. The man who had brought all of this about . . . Sam being appointed a U.S. marshal . . . the chase after Bilo Mackley . . . their coming back with the hardcase so's he could testify and put an end to the judge's crooked ways.

Around a fat cigar Kiley Glover said smugly, "This is the only way to travel."

"How's the shoulder?"

"Only twinges when someone starts jawing about hosses and long rides."

"How about you, Sam," Joe McVay said, "you glad to be heading back?"

"That and a little worried."

"About what Judge Garth'll do when he sees Mackley here?"

"He won't be happy, I'll tell you. But we're just doing our job."

"Reckon so. Job—ain't that something you've been avoiding all these years?"

This brought a smile from Sam Chapman. "Come to think of it, work isn't all that bad."

A stiff wind sent dust scudding across the street and around buildings when a stagecoach pulled up before the Wells Fargo building. Striding out to meet the passengers was the editor of the *Yellowstone Journal.* Sam Chapman, the last passenger to clamber down, shook the outstretched hand of Thompson R. McElrath. "Glad you could make it," said Sam.

"First time I've been to Big Timber—a thriving community. And this must be why I'm here." T.R. McElrath glanced over at Bilo Mackley being hustled under the covered porch by Joe McVay.

"So far I haven't told anyone you were coming, T.R."

"Much as I dislike stagecoaches," stated the editor of the *Yellowstone Journal,* "this was a trip I had to make. Now I suppose the rest is up to your prisoner."

"The Randall Hotel is just upstreet. And it's nooning."

"Yes, perhaps a good meal will put Mr. Mackley in a talking mood. At any rate, Sam, I'll spring for dinner."

They fell in behind Glover and McVay walking between Bilo Mackley. But they separated in the dining room of the Randall Hotel, the deputy marshals taking a window table as Sam brought his prisoner to a back table, and where Mackley asked, "Don't you put out that newspaper back at Miles City?"

"I'm its editor." McElrath watched as Sam removed the handcuffs, then McElrath held out his hand and introduced himself.

There was some hesitation on Mackley's part before he forced an uneasy smile and shook the editor's hand. "You're figuring to get a story out of me." It was a grim declaration more than a question, and in Bilo Mackley's eyes glittered distrust and just a shade of fear. For he knew what being brought to Miles City meant.

Sam caught a waitress's eye, and from her ordered beers around, as she informed them the menu for the day was up on the back wall of the spacious dining room. As she went away, he said, "Bilo, we went to a lot of trouble not only finding you but saving your life."

"Just so's you could bring me back to be hung."

"The court will decide that."

"Meaning Judge Garth," he sneered.

"We're hoping," pitched in McElrath, "your testimony will help put the judge where he belongs, in territorial prison. Or, from what I've learned from Marshal Chapman, a hanging sentence."

"Garth deserves that, and worse," agreed the hardcase as the waitress returned with three steins of beer balanced on a tray. After being handed one of the steins, Mackley downed his in several thirsty gulps. "I could use a refill, and maybe some whiskey."

"Beer will do for all of us," Sam told him. "Okay, Bilo, what we want is a statement from you implicating Judge Garth in the murder of rancher George Davine."

"Yeah, I give you this statement," he blustered, "and once we get back to Miles City . . . well, the judge has a way of taking out people."

"This is why Mr. McElrath is here. Any statement you make will be printed in the *Yellowstone*

234

Journal. Once it's in there, I bring you back to Miles City. The power of the press, Bilo, will protect you."

"One way of looking at it," he pondered.

"Once I have your statement implicating Judge Garth, I'll take the afternoon stage back. What you tell me will be in tomorrow's edition of the *Yellowstone Journal.* Day after tomorrow Sam will bring you back. By then most everyone in Miles City will be wanting to form a lynch mob."

"Suits me, if they hang Garth."

"Awright, Bilo, did you or the judge kill that rancher?"

"I helped Garth, no question about that. But it was Grath's pistola that did the job. Buried him south along the river."

T.R. McElrath had taken out a pad of paper and a large wooden pencil, and he placed on paper Bilo Mackley's exact words. "If you would be so kind as to give me some more details . . ."

Their meals, brought by the same waitress, were getting cold by the time the hardcase had given a detailed accounting of just how George Davine had been murdered. With his mouth set in grim lines, Mackley signed his name to the document. And it was now that Sam Chapman said, "There's one other thing, Bilo."

"Reckon I know what that is, Chapman. Why I did in that girl working for Mag Burns. Well, there's more than one Garth that's gonna get hung. Those other whores done in . . . well, not this hombre. Rye Garth killed them. I was there." An evil grin lifted the hardcase's mouth and eyes. "Rye paid me to kill that girl of Mag's. Should never have let him talk me into doing it."

"Because he wanted to use you as a scapegoat," agreed Sam.

"Editor, I made one statement," he said flatly. "Might as well make another. As for me killing that girl, had a hard time living with myself afterward. Can't bring her back. But know I've got to answer for it. So fire away, editor, ask me what I know about Rye."

Thursday, two days after the editor of the *Yellowstone Journal* had taken his departure for Miles City, once again Sam Chapman found himself about to board a stagecoach for the final leg of a long journey. Only this time there were other passengers, two women with bold eyes and an equal number of carpetbaggers bound for the same destination. Right away Sam knew there was going to be trouble when one of the carpetbaggers noticed the handcuffs around Milo Mackley's wrists.

"That convict isn't riding with us."

The man riding shotgun, a grizzled coot with a patch over one eye, replied, "Marshal's bought a ticket for him; he's entitled to his share of that stagecoach."

"Then he's gonna ride up on top with you."

"Aren't you Fresno Oldham?"

Hefting his Winchester, along with giving Sam an appraising eye, shotgun Fresno Oldham said, "I be him. Word has it that you gunned down Tonto Blair."

236

"Tonto Blair had the misfortune to tangle with a silvertip."

"Tonto deserved that, and more."

"There's eight of us and that coach will only hold six passengers."

"No problem, Marshal Chapman." Oldham swung on the carpetbagger. "You, and you, climb up and perch on top."

The carpetbagger stiffened before replying, "I will not be spoken to that way. Neither will Clyde here."

"Then we'll be leaving without you or Clyde."

"Why . . . I never . . ."

"Obliged," Sam said softly to the shotgun. He stood by the open door as the women clambered up first, then his deputies and Bilo Mackley. When it was Sam's turn to enter, he found himself seated between the women, both of whom seemed determined to sit as close to him as possible. And for this he had to endure the grins of Glover and McVay. Even Bilo Mackley forced a smile at this turn of events.

When they'd been out on the main trail for a couple of hours, Bilo Mackley lighted a cigarillo, and took a long drag from it before saying, "Sure would like to see a copy of the *Yellowstone Journal*."

"Betcha," said Joe McVay, "our old friend, Judge Garth, is really trying to explain this away."

"I'm hoping Garth will be gone when we get to Miles City."

"Thought you wanted to arrest him?"

"I do. But either Judge Garth will take a powder, or . . ."

"Or what, Sam?"

"Lay an ambush for us."

"Never considered something like that."

"Garth knows the game is up. But like that silvertip that got Tonto Blair, he might try most anything."

"Where does that leave me?"

Sam stared Bilo Mackley in the eyes, and to a reassuring smile he said, "Like us, Bilo, trying to square things. You've got us, and if you think about it, everyone at Miles City backing our play."

To which Joe McVay added, "What more can any of us ask."

Chapter Twenty-two

Scarcely had the sun begun its western descent when the headlines in the *Yellowstone Journal* seemed to hold back the dark encroachments of night. The big bold headlines scrawled across the front page proclaimed it best:

HARLAN AND RYE GARTH ACCUSED OF MURDER

Sprawled below in cryptic detail were the accusing words of gunhand Bilo Mackley as recorded by T.R. McElrath over at Big Timber. Omitted by the editor of the *Yellowstone Journal* were no gory details. First there was the account of how George Davine had been murdered, this awful deed done by federal judge Garth. Just as damning followed the telling in the newspaper of how Rye Garth had seemingly killed without remorse.

A couple of hours later, the newspaper being rushed out into the streets of Miles City around four that afternoon, the public was clamoring for more copies as townsfolk gathered on the streets or talked about the damning news over beers or coffee.

At the 44, Mag Burns voiced what a lot of

people were wondering, "Where is Marshal Sam Chapman and his prisoner, Bilo Mackley?"

Mag was up and about now, but the prolonged absence of Sam had given her a lot of time to think. She was fond of Sam. Whether she loved him or not was another question. A few years ago, Mag might have even proposed to him. Sam had spoken of his failed marriages, and she of the one time she'd been married to a Denver socialite. Perhaps it was better that they kept things as they were, though Sam made her feel awful good when he came around.

Over at the Inter Ocean Hotel, where T.R. McElrath was holding court, a lot of businessmen and a couple of ranchers, and a major from Fort Keogh, were also questioning the whereabouts of U.S. Marshal Chapman.

"He'll be here, gentlemen."

"If he doesn't show, T.R., it could be you'll be the one Judge Garth throws in that jail of his."

"What I'm reading here still boggles my mind. Not only had the judge committed murder, but that son of his, Rye, has been killing these girls. Both of them accused of doing this by a known gunhand."

"I have Bilo Mackley's statements to back up my newspaper."

"This part in here, T.R., as told by Marshal Chapman as to how our sheriff got himself killed over at Silver Gate. Chapman blandly states that Judge Garth ordered Pindale to kill Mackley."

"I know Pindale—rather I knew that Toby Pindale may not be much as a sheriff—but to do murder for Judge Garth?"

240

"Yes, I know that without Marshal Chapman here to back up my story you find what you're reading hard to swallow. Chapman will be here. Probably today, or even tomorrow, but he'll show."

The haggard eyes of Judge Harlan A. Garth went again to the front page of the *Yellowstone Journal* spread out on his desk. This morning he had come to work in fine fettle, and looking forward to presiding over his courtroom. Swept from his mind had been any thoughts of the past, even the recent murder of banker Charley Miller. Just yesterday morning he'd discussed with Rye the need to buy more cattle and perhaps increase the holdings of the Clearwater by buying land adjoining it to the northwest. Briefly, there'd been some concern over whether or not that gunfighter he'd hired and Sheriff Pindale had found Mackley.

Presently the *Yellowstone Journal* told him otherwise. Every so often he'd push up from his desk and hurry to a window, there to scan the western approaches to Miles City for any sign of the lawmen bringing in Bilo Mackley. He couldn't help noticing also the way people would stand and stare over at the courthouse. What was printed here had made him a pariah, had damned him in the eyes of everyone here. Even his clerks couldn't look him in the eye, and angrily he'd ordered them out of the building.

In a lower desk drawer was a gunbelt. Should he buckle it on and head west to intercept Marshal Chapman? But what could he do against Chapman

241

and his deputy marshals? This newspaper was damning enough. When Bilo Mackley arrived and started spieling out what he knew, Harlan Garth realized his days as a judge were over.

"It can't end this way! Dammit . . . it can't." He crumpled the newspaper up and tossed it into a quiet corner. And again he sought the whiskey bottle resting on a cabinet. The shaking hands of Judge Garth poured whiskey into a glass as he struggled inwardly for a way out of this.

After Mackley had fled, Harlan Garth had given the other hardcases their walking papers. A mistake, he realized. Morning passed into early afternoon as he centered his reeling thoughts on the one person who had brought all of this about.

"My son . . . because of Rye murdering those whores. Rye, damn you, you've brought ruin upon us."

Then he spun toward an open window when he heard a passerby below on the boardwalk shout that the stagecoach was coming in from the west. He spotted it coming in on the flats south of the river. Before it had been all anger and numbed disbelief. He tracked the stagecoach with spearing eyes until the span of six horses swept it behind the outlying buildings. A short time later it reappeared on the northern end of Main Street, to have onlookers surge out into the street after it. Instead of drawing up before the stagecoach office, the driver reined his horses on to wheel over and brake to a halt before the city jail. Two women emerged first.

"Perhaps . . . perhaps Mackley isn't on the stage, that McElrath's story is a damnable lie."

242

The crumbling hopes of Judge Garth faded away when Marshal Chapman emerged from the stage-coach brandishing a rifle, and likewise the deputy marshals, Glover and McVay. Now an intense pain exploded behind the eyes of Harlan Garth when the one man who could send him to the gallows clambered out of the stagecoach.

"Mackley! No . . . he should be dead . . ."

Somehow, blindly, Harlan A. Garth found himself spinning away from the window toward his coat hanging from a rack by the closed door. He grabbed his coat and shrugged into it, and reached for his hat as he remembered the gun in his desk. When he'd strapped this about his waist, Garth stumbled out of his office and found the back stairway. Outside, he hurried toward his lonely and big house on the outskirts of Miles City. And from there he saddled a horse, and scrambling aboard it, spurred it desperately along a southward-flowing lane and toward the Clearwater.

"Rye . . . damn you . . . it's all your fault!"

"When we left," commented Kiley Glover, "it was just that fire-eating preacher seeing us off."

"Now the whole town is here."

"All because of McElrath and his *Yellowstone Journal*," said Marshal Sam Chapman.

It was there, Sam couldn't help noticing, in their eyes and the way they stood, a naked respect for him and the deputy marshals. He felt different too, as if all of these people crowding the street had come to pay homage to an honest lawman. No

243

longer did he feel like a drifter, but a man somehow finding his place out here. Not that he had any great ambitions to continue on as a U.S. marshal. Then T.R. McElrath was shouldering up and coming to stand by Sam.

"I've just won myself a few bets."

"How's that."

The editor said, "From those who were betting you wouldn't show."

Hefting his rifle, Sam nodded at the city jail and one of Sheriff Pindale's deputies. "Standish, I'm placing my prisoner in your care."

"Why," questioned the deputy, "not take him over to the courthouse."

"Because there's still the matter of arresting Judge Garth."

"A wise decision."

"Best I could come up with at the moment, T.R." He watched as Glover and McVay brought Bilo Mackley onto the boardwalk and through the open doorway of the jail. "There go some good men."

"Marshal," someone called out, "is it the truth what's printed in the *Yellowstone Journal?*"

In a voice pitched so that it carried to the fringes of those filling the street and boardwalks Sam replied, "Sometimes justice is slow out here. Sometimes the law is corrupted by those sworn to uphold it. I was there, in Silver Gate, when Toby Pindale got gunned down. It was plain that Toby and a gunfighter hired by Judge Garth meant to see that Bilo Mackley never got back here to testify against Garth. So, yup, that statement by Mackley is the Gospel truth."

244

Sam cleared his throat as he thumbed back his Stetson. "This badge I'm wearing . . . now after what's happened I understand it more — what it means. That it's an honor to be toting it, and an honor to uphold the law for the folks hereabouts." Brusquely he pivoted around, and followed by the editor of the *Yellowstone Journal,* went into the jail office.

Placing his rifle on the desk, Sam nodded at the cup of coffee Joe McVay was holding out. "Obliged, Joe. How's the shoulder, Kiley?"

"Coming along."

"As of this moment I'm releasing you boys of any obligations holding you to wearing those badges."

"Lookee, here, Marshal Chapman, we've come this far with Bilo Mackley. And we aim to keep wearing these badges until Mackley's trial is over with and Judge Garth is put away."

"Okay, okay," Sam said, and smiling. "Seems you've been weaned into becoming starpackers. But now I've got to take a walk."

"Want me to come along?"

"No, Joe, what I'm about to do will give me a lot of pleasure."

"Garth won't go easily."

"If I recollect, Harlan Garth always has others doing his dirty work. Once I've got Garth in Basement Felony, I figure it'll be okay to bring Mackley over there." Then he took the time to drain his cup before handing it back to McVay and leaving.

There were still a lot of people standing along the street when Sam Chapman appeared. When they realized Sam was heading south along the street with the intention of going to the courthouse, most of them followed, but at a safe distance. Back there, he'd spotted Mag Burns in the crowd, caught her eyes for the briefest of moments, and was relieved to see how well she looked. "Sure will be good to catch up on things at the 44."

As he came around that last building and viewed the large courthouse standing well back from the street amongst oak and elm trees, Sam Chapman slowed a little. Certainly Harlan Garth had read the *Yellowstone Journal*. But he doubted that even as arrogant and disdainful as Garth was, the man wouldn't stay around and suffer the humiliation of being arrested. He went on, and then when Sam stepped onto the walkway leading up the the front doors, through them stepped jailer Ham Lauden and clerk of court Otis Plumb. Right away he knew Judge Garth had fled.

"Welcome back, Marshal Chapman."

"Glad to be back, Ham."

Otis Plumb said, "According to territorial law, Sam, you're now in charge of things . . . this courthouse and all that it surveys. That is, until a new judge arrives. Last I saw of Judge Garth, he was breaking out the back door. He could be at his house."

"Doubt that, Otis. You holding any prisoners?"

"Basement Felony is empty."

"That'll change before long, Ham. Garth, I figure he headed out to the Clearwater. So I'll be needing a horse."

"You're not going out there by yourself?"

246

"Just earning my pay, Otis. And do me a favor, head over to the city jail and tell my deputies to bring Milo Mackley over here. Keep a light in the window for me, boys."

Chapter Twenty-three

Sam Chapman had been riding on Clearwater land for about an hour when suddenly he accosted four riders coming over a rise in the road. He recognized Clearwater foreman Phil Brady, realized there wouldn't be any trouble when Brady called out to him.

"I can't figure it, Marshal Chapman," said Brady as he reined up while the others hung back some. "The judge riding out and firing all of us."

"Judge Garth is still out there?"

"When I left he was arguing with Rye."

"That so?"

"Never seen the judge like this before. Almost as though he didn't know me, or these others. We were just riding out—maybe a mile or two away from the home buildings—when I heard this muffled sound."

"A gunshot?"

"Figured it was. But let the Garths tear one another apart for all I care." The foreman touched spurs to his horse as did the other cowpunchers.

And Sam went the opposite way but spurring to a canter. This could only mean it was showdown time for the Garths. The sun was sinking below the western ramparts when he sighted the main buildings. Light was showing in the sprawling ranchhouse, and Sam rode up warily. A man such as Harlan A. Garth wouldn't come out and draw against him, for he figured Garth's style was more that of an ambusher. Tying the reins to a low branch of an elm, Sam unleathered his Smith & Wesson as he slipped around to the back entrance. As one boot touched onto the porch steps, a creaking noise from behind brought Sam around in a crouch.

"Do . . . not shoot . . ."

Sam's finger eased its pressure on the trigger as he blurted out angrily, "A man can get himself killed doing that." He stared at the Chinese cook framed in light pouring out of his log cabin.

"You are a lawman?"

"A U.S. Marshal."

"Evil things have happened," said Li Wong as Sam moved over. "The father comes home this afternoon, marshal. There are bad words between father and son. Fearing what is to come, I flee to my cabin. I tell my wife to pack our things for we shall leave this evil place. Then . . . then, marshal, just a little while ago, a gun is fired."

"Are Judge Garth and his son still in the house?"

Li Wong pointed to the big hip-roofed barn set to the northeast.

Nodding, Sam said, "Can't blame you for pulling the pin and hightailing it out of here. And I'm obliged for you helping me."

Warily Marshal Sam Chapman went at a trot across the open yard until he passed a large pole corral occupied by several horses. In the dying shards of sunlight still poking down at the Clearwater from the west Sam could see that one of the front double doors stood open, and as he got closer, through the open door came the voice of Judge Harlan A. Garth. And while easing along the front wall Sam suddenly noticed the saddled horse wheeling about just outside another pole corral, the reins dangling by its forelegs, the bronc acting skittish, and with its eyes showing its fear.

Again came Judge Garth's voice pitched in anger, "Therefore, Rye Garth, by the power vested in me as territorial judge I sentence you to be hanged by the neck until dead!"

Only when Sam Chapman snaked a look into the barn did he realize to his shocked surprise that the sentence had been carried out. For swaying at the end of a rope snugged around a high rafter was the body of Rye Garth. The back door faced to the west, and it stood open, letting in rays of reddish sunlight that seemed to center on Rye Garth. Even more shocking to Sam was Judge Garth seated on a chair in the center aisle, and wearing one of his judicial black robes, the hand hanging down by his left side grasping a sixgun. Now, when Garth spoke again, it came to Sam Chapman that his voice seemed uneven, as though the judge was fighting back his grief over having hung his son.

"Don't make me use this gun, Judge Garth!" Sam warned as he stepped warily down the center aisle.

"Bailiff," spoke up Judge Garth as though he hadn't heard Marshal Chapman, "take the prisoner out to the gallows." The gun dropped out of Harlan

Garth's hand.

Then Sam was kicking the gun into a gutter and easing around to face Judge Garth. What he saw sickened him, the blood staining the front of the white shirt under the open robe, the yellowish tint to the skin and those eyes still pouring out all of the hatred for his son. He figured that Garth had shot himself after hanging his son, Rye. Somewhere along the line Judge Garth's mind must have snapped to make him do this.

"Judge . . . it's me, Sam Chapman . . ."

"Chapman?" His voice was more raspy now, and with his shattered lungs trying to suck in more air as his gravely wounded body fought to stay alive. "Marshal Sam Chapman?"

"You haven't got long—no more'n a half hour, Judge Garth."

"Chapman . . . don't just stand there . . . take the prisoner out to the gallows. Then hang him!" Then he went slack in the chair as his head folded down onto his sunken chest.

With a sorrowful shake of his head, Sam Chapman leathered his Smith & Wesson. He stood there for a while staring at the man who'd caused so much pain for others. Sam knew that he would never figure out why a man of such brilliance would turn to killing. Or the son, for that matter.

It wasn't until the following morning that Sam Chapman brought his horse away from the mounds of reddish dirt marking a hillside. After burying both Harlan Garth and his son, Sam found that he couldn't say any Christian words over their graves. Only when he let his horse pick its way up a flowing rise in the lane did Sam draw up to look back, and he framed these words, "How you died, Judge Garth, is stranger than how you lived. But when I get back to Miles City the truth will have to come out. Guess . . . guess this badge I'm packing has something to do with that."

POWELL'S ARMY
BY TERENCE DUNCAN

#1: UNCHAINED LIGHTNING   (1994, $2.50)

Thundering out of the past, a trio of deadly enforcers dispenses its own brand of frontier justice throughout the untamed American West! Two men and one woman, they are the U.S. Army's most lethal secret weapon — they are POWELL'S ARMY!

#2: APACHE RAIDERS   (2073, $2.50)

The disappearance of seventeen Apache maidens brings tribal unrest to the violent breaking point. To prevent an explosion of bloodshed, Powell's Army races through a nightmare world south of the border — and into the deadly clutches of a vicious band of Mexican flesh merchants!

#3: MUSTANG WARRIORS   (2171, $2.50)

Someone is selling cavalry guns and horses to the Comanche — and that spells trouble for the bluecoats' campaign against Chief Quanah Parker's bloodthirsty Kwahadi warriors. But Powell's Army are no strangers to trouble. When the showdown comes, they'll be ready — and someone is going to die!

#4: ROBBERS ROOST   (2285, $2.50)

After hijacking an army payroll wagon and killing the troopers riding guard, Three-Fingered Jack and his gang high-tail it into Virginia City to spend their ill-gotten gains. But Powell's Army plans to apprehend the murderous hardcases before the local vigilantes do — to make sure that Jack and his slimy band stretch hemp the legal way!

THE SURVIVALIST SERIES
by Jerry Ahern